Published in 2016 by Enslow Publishing, LLC
101 W. 23rd Street, Suite 240, New York, NY 10011

Copyright (c) 2016 by Enslow Publishing, LLC.

All rights reserved.

No part of this book may be reproduced by any means without the written permission of the publisher.

Library of Congress Cataloging-in-Publication Data

Names: Hanson-Harding, Alexandra, author.
Title: Are you being racially profiled? / Alexandra Hanson-Harding.
Description: New York, NY : Enslow Publishing, [2016] | Series: Got issues? | Includes bibliographical references and index.
Identifiers: LCCN 2015038955 | ISBN 9780766071384
Subjects: LCSH: Racial profiling in law enforcement--United States--Juvenile literature. | Discrimination in law enforcement--United States--Juvenile literature. | Race discrimination--United States--Juvenile literature.
Classification: LCC HV7936.R3 H358 2016 | DDC 363.2/308900973--dc23
LC record available at http://lccn.loc.gov/2015038955

Printed in the United States of America

To Our Readers: We have done our best to make sure all website addresses in this book were active and appropriate when we went to press. However, the author and the publisher have no control over and assume no liability for the material available on those websites or on any websites they may link to. Any comments or suggestions can be sent by e-mail to customerservice@enslow.com.

For many of the images in this book, the people photographed are models. The depictions do not imply actual situations or events.

Photo Credits: Cover, p. 1 PathDoc/Shutterstock.com; p. 4 ©iStockphoto.com/digitalskillet; p. 6 Mark Bonifacio/NY Daily News/Getty Images; p. 9 Patrick Smith/Getty Images North America/Getty Images; p. 10 Don Smetzer/The Image Bank/Getty Images; p. 12 AFP/Getty Images; p. 14 ©iStockphoto.com/IPGGutenburgUKLtd; p. 17 © RosaIreneBetancourt 3/Alamy Stock Photo; p. 19 Robert Nickelsberg/Getty Images North America/Getty Images; p. 22 © Norma Jean Gargasz/Alamy Stock Photo; p. 23 Digital Vision/Photodisc/Thinkstock; p. 24 © Richard Levine/Alamy Stock Photo; p. 26 Lihee Avidan/Photolibrary/Getty Images; p. 28 SAUL LOEB/AFP/Getty Images; p. 32 man Mountain biking; p. 34 Schmidt_Alex/Shutterstock.com; p. 35 Stockbyte/Thinkstock; p. 37 James Devaney/GC Images/Getty Images; p. 39 Joe Raedle/Getty Images News/Getty Images; p. 41 Phil Velasquez/Chicago Tribune/TNS/Getty Images; p. 44 iStock/Izabela Habur; p. 46 Bilgin S. Sasmaz/Anadolu Agency/Getty Images; p. 48 Ann Hermes/The Christian Science Monitor/Getty Images; p. 51 © AP Photo; p. 53 monkeybusinessimages/iStock/Thinkstock; p. 55 somsak suwanput/Shutterstock.com; p. 57 pio3/Shutterstock.com; p. 59 Michael B. Thomas/AFP/Getty Images; p. 61 © Fox/Courtesy: Everett Collection; p. 64 lev radin/Shutterstock.com; p. 66 Stokkete/Shutterstock.com; p. 68 LUCAS JACKSON/Reuters/Landov; p. 71 Axel Bueckert/Shutterstock.com; p. 73 Design-Pics/Design-Pics/Superstock.com; p. 74 Ann Hermes/The Christian Science Monitor/Getty Images; p.76 josefkubes/iStock/Thinkstock; p. 77 Gary Friedman/Los Angeles Times/Getty Images; p. 78 Gianni Ferrari/Cover/Getty Images; p. 81 Anne Cusack/Los Angeles Times/Getty Images; p. 84 SAUL LOEB/AFP/Getty Images; p. 85 AAraujo/Shutterstock.com; p. 87 Nabil K. Mark/Centre Daily Times/TNS/Getty Images; p. 90 DON EMMERT/AFP/Getty Images; p. 92.

Contents

Chapter 1	The Talk	4
Chapter 2	What Is Racial Profiling?	14
Chapter 3	On the Street	23
Chapter 4	Racial Profiling in Cars and Planes	34
Chapter 5	The School to Prison Pipeline	44
Chapter 6	Police Overreach?	55
Chapter 7	Juvenile Injustice	66
Chapter 8	Prisons	76
Chapter 9	Fighting Against Racial Profiling	85
	Chapter Notes	94
	Glossary	104
	For More Information	106
	Further Reading	109
	Index	110

1
The Talk

Amy Hunter thought she and her husband, a federal law enforcement officer, had prepared her twin sons for lives as young African American men. "We promised ourselves we would give our kids 'The Talk' when they were as tall as I am—I'm five feet tall. So when they were ten, we fully explained that though they were children, there were certain people that wouldn't see them as children anymore . . . that there are penalties and consequences for them that there aren't for white children."

But the St. Louis, Missouri, mother and Diversity Educator still wasn't prepared for what happened one day when one of the boys, Ashton, was twelve. Her son went to hang out with friends at a frozen yogurt place. As he was walking home, he saw a police car drive by. Then he saw it again, circling around. "Sure enough," she said, "five houses away from home, they stopped him."

The Talk

The officers made Ashton assume the position and put his hands on the hood of the police car while they searched him. They made him empty his pockets and explain who he was and where he was going. When he asked why he was being searched, the twelve-year-old was told that he fit the description of a criminal on the loose—a grown man wielding a machete. Amy said:

> He comes home to me from private school, and he's flustered. He goes to private school; this is not like anything he's seen. He's incredibly flustered. He asks, "Why did they stop me? I'm wearing khakis and a polo shirt and it's tucked in. I'm wearing Docksiders." He was convinced that he would be stopped only if he was dressed a certain way.
>
> He asks, "Did it happen because it was I was black?"
>
> I answer, "I don't know."
>
> He says, "I thought of running home to you. I was only five houses away."
>
> And then, my heart stopped. Because I thought I had remembered everything. But I hadn't. I forgot to tell him *not to run*.
>
> At this point, there are tears at bottom of his eyes. He asks me, "Mommy, I just want to know—how long this will last?"
>
> By now, I'm crying, too. I say, "Forever."[1]

The police have a scary job. They have to go out and look for dangerous people—such as grown men with machetes. But Ashton was not a grown man. He did not have a machete. Why was he stopped? Would he have been treated the same way if he were white? It is impossible to know why Ashton was stopped that day. Police are allowed a wide latitude in hunting down potential criminals.

Are You Being Racially Profiled?

Police officers in the United States are statistically more likely to detain blacks, Latinos, Muslims, and Native Americans than they are whites. In addition, people of color regularly receive harsher penalties than whites who have committed the same crimes.

Statistics show that African Americans, Latinos, Native Americans, Muslims, and various other racial, ethnic, and religious groups in the United States are stopped by the police, arrested, and harassed by law enforcement officers more often than whites. They are also charged with crimes more often than whites and receive harsher sentences than white citizens who have committed the same crimes. One stop, one arrest, and one conviction at a time, numbers are telling a story in this country. As President Barack Obama said, "The bottom line is that in too many places, black boys and black men, Latino boys and Latino men experience being treated differently under the law."[2] When this happens, it is called racial profiling.

As unfair as it might be for people of color to be arrested and harassed, there is an even greater sense of fear that strikes the hearts of their families. These families worry that their young people are in danger of violence or even death—not at the hands of criminals but at the hands of law enforcement officers.

Karen Eagle, a Lakota mother of a teenage boy, Miguel, said she's so frightened that her son will be shot down by police that she doesn't want him to walk around with more than two friends at a time. She's afraid that if he does, the police will think he's in a gang. She tells him always to treat the police with respect. If they're rude, she says, just "eat it." Why? As she told *Al Jazeera*, "I would rather have a whole healthy alive son and help him heal from that indignity rather than bury my son," she said. "I'm very disappointed I have to arm my son with that knowledge."[3]

She has reason to be cautious. Native Americans make up 0.8 percent of the population but average 1.9 percent of those killed by police. Meanwhile, African Americans make up 13 percent of the population and average 26 percent of police killings. That makes Native Americans the ethnic group most likely to be killed by the police in the United States.[4]

The Slap Heard Around the World

In April 2015, Toya Graham, an African American mother from Baltimore, Maryland, saw something on the news she did not want to see: her sixteen-year-old son, Michael, in the middle of a protest against the police after the death of Freddie Gray. Graham rushed to the site of the protest, slapped her son, and furiously dragged him away. The moment was caught on video, shown on TV, and widely discussed. Graham was both criticized and praised widely for her strictness. Her act was called "the slap that was heard around the world." Michael was embarrassed, but ultimately he understood. "She didn't want me to get in trouble [with the] law. She didn't want me to be like another Freddie Gray," he said on CNN.[5]

In April 2015, twenty-five-year-old Freddie Gray was arrested in Baltimore. Police officers said he was carrying what they called an illegal switchblade knife. They took him to jail in a police van. But by the time Gray arrived at the jail, he had gone limp. His spine had been severed. He went into a coma. A week later, he was dead.

Afterward, protests and riots broke out in the city. Many in Baltimore were furious at the rough treatment Freddie Gray had received from the arresting officers. Baltimore police have had a difficult history with the city's largely black population. The police department has been sued successfully in the past for giving rough rides to people who have been arrested and put in police vans. Rough rides are when handcuffed suspects are not buckled into their seats and the driver slams on the brakes to cause pain or injury. In fact, between 2012 and 2015, Baltimore's city jail refused more than 2,600 detainees because they were brought with injuries too severe to allow them to be admitted, according to records uncovered by *The Baltimore Sun*.[6]

> Stories of this frightening practice spread, which made citizens afraid and distrustful of the police. But this distrust was nothing new. Baltimore had long been a poverty-stricken city with a high crime rate. Television shows, such as

The Talk

Thousands of demonstrators marched from Baltimore's City Hall to protest the death of Freddie Gray in 2015. Gray's death came as a result of a severe spinal cord injury he received while being taken into police custody.

Homicide and *The Wire*, depicted its grim murders. It needed some serious help. In 2005, Democratic Mayor Martin O'Malley tried to clean up Baltimore, but his solution was extreme. During that year, 100,000 of Baltimore's 640,000 citizens—almost one out of every six of its mostly black men, women, and children—were arrested. Three quarters were arrested without a warrant. A third of those people were let go without charges. The crime rate did drop—but at the cost of the public's faith in the police and their fairness.[7]

A New Urgency

Recently, racial profiling has become a charged topic. Story after story, such as the death of Freddie Gray, has appeared in the news. Not only have they made many families of color anxious about the safety of their children, they have also led to many critical discussions

Parents of nonwhite children bear the burden of educating their kids about potential run-ins with police.

of the police, which has led to police officers feeling scrutinized and uncomfortable.

Are there more incidents of racial profiling than there were in the past? It is hard to know. One thing that is clearly different, however, is that cameras—surveillance cameras, police body cams, cameras in police cruisers, and cellphone cameras—have been capturing some shocking examples of citizens being harmed by law enforcement officials. When those images have appeared on the Internet, they have made a horrifying reality impossible to ignore. As painful as those images are to view, they have helped young activists find their voices and new ways to express their hunger for change by writing articles and using social media, such as Twitter, to disseminate ideas about civil rights.

Land of the Free?

The United States has always been a nation that prides itself on being the land of the free. According to its Constitution, US citizens are "endowed with certain inalienable rights"—that is, rights no one can take away because you are human. But the nation has not always lived up to its promise. Luckily, there have been individuals throughout the nation's history who believed in the notion of freedom and have fought for the United States to become a more just society. That is still true today.

Could racial profiling happen to you? If you're a person of color, there is unfortunately no guarantee that you will not be profiled. But you don't have to feel afraid and hopeless. In this resource, you will learn how to decrease your chances of being racially profiled. You will also learn about your legal rights in the event that you are a victim of racial profiling. You will learn what exactly racial profiling is and that it takes place in such places as school, the street, cars, and court. You will learn about the unfairness of the Prison-Industrial Complex that imprisons a higher rate of people of color than whites for similar crimes.

Are You Being Racially Profiled?

Many look back to the work of Martin Luther King Jr. and other leaders of the 1960s Civil Rights Movement. But we are still fighting for civil rights today, as evidenced by protests in Baltimore, Maryland; Ferguson, Missouri; and beyond.

But you will also learn why you should be hopeful and how young people have the power to change the world in ways they never have before. You will learn ways that everyone—victims, friends, families, and allies—can join the fight for awareness of this epidemic of unfairness hiding in plain sight and how you can join in what many are calling the second Civil Rights Movement that is sweeping the nation. As Amy Hunter says, "I'm not asking people to get used to racial profiling. I'm asking for people to change it. I can imagine a day when people aren't profiled. We have a history of changing. And I know America can change for the better."[8]

2

What Is Racial Profiling?

Jonathan Williams is an African American man who works as a recreation therapist at a hospital in New Jersey. One day, an announcement over the hospital loudspeaker warned people who normally parked their cars in a certain lot to move them to make room for a fund-raiser. Williams rushed out to move his car, and there in the parking lot was a police cruiser. When the officer spotted him, Jon got nervous.

> As I got in my car, I got the vibe. The policeman was totally checking me out. Sure enough he gets out of his police car, walks over to me, and goes, "Can I see your driver's license and registration."
>
> "Why?" I ask.
>
> He just continues, "You ever been in Camden?" [Camden is a predominantly African American city several hours away.]

"No."

"You have a tattoo on your left arm?" he asks.

"No."

"Would you mind rolling up your sleeve?"

I'm wearing a fleece. It's tight, and I have a hard time pushing up the sleeves. But he can't wait for one second till I do. He grabs my arm and starts shoving the sleeve up my arm for me.

"Excuse me," I say, "I can do this."

My (white) friend Toni comes over, and she says, "Officer, I know him, leave him alone!" and (finally) the officer backs off. Finally I roll the sleeve up, and show him—no tattoo. But I'm thinking, *You can't tell one black man from another?*[1]

Differences in Definition

So what is racial profiling? Definitions can vary. According to the American Civil Liberties Union (ACLU), racial profiling occurs when law enforcement officials choose whom to investigate for a crime based on the individual's race, religion, ethnic background, or country of origin. Racial profiling can include using race to decide which drivers to stop for small traffic violations or which pedestrians to search for illegal drugs. It can also affect who is stopped at airports or border crossings. And it can come into play in who gets charged with crimes for similar offenses and how serious sentences are for those same crimes. Racial profiling can happen in schools, as well.

Racial profiling is not the legitimate search for a specific suspect who belongs to a certain race or ethnicity. It means targeting people because they belong to a certain race or ethnicity. Different groups can have different meanings for what racial profiling is, however. For instance, the city of San Jose, California, used to have a narrow definition of what racial profiling was. An officer was only violating a civilian's rights by racially profiling that person if the officer first "stopped an individual solely because of race, gender or other bias." But in 2011, they changed the circumstance to make it a violation for an officer to show racially biased behavior at any time during an encounter with a civilian. Independent police auditor LaDoris Cordell gave an example of possibly biased policing, "If an officer has a Latino man sit on the curb, then would the officer have a white man in a suit sit on a curb, if the circumstances were the same?"[2]

Another definition of racial profiling comes from a different California city. A 2008 Yale study of the Los Angeles Police Department (LAPD) discovered that officers stopped blacks and Latinos for frisks, searches, and arrests at much higher rates than they did whites, whether they lived in high-crime areas or not. But the LAPD police chief at the time, William Bratton, resisted the idea that racial profiling was taking place, saying, "We cannot climb inside the head of the officers."[3] In other words, Bratton suggested that it was impossible to know the officers' intentions when they arrested a particular individual, therefore it was almost impossible to say whether an officer was engaged in racial profiling.

The public was unhappy with Bratton's comment. Many people filed complaints. Finally, the US Justice Department gathered a team of investigators who concentrated not on the officers' thought processes but on the the constitutional rights of people who filed complaints against the police department. That's when they discovered patterns of abuse by certain officers. It didn't help the LAPD when the Justice Department got hold of a tape where two officers admitted they couldn't do their jobs without racially profiling. In 2012, The LAPD decided for the first time that motorcycle officer Patrick Smith had pulled over a large number of Latinos then tried to hide that fact by classifying them as white on his paperwork.[4]

What Is Racial Profiling?

On its website, the American Civil Liberties Union (ACLU) defines racial profiling as the targeting of people of color "based on perceived race, ethnicity, national origin, or religion."

Why Racial Profiling is a Problem

You might ask, "What's the big deal about racial profiling? Does it actually hurt anyone?" The truth is, racial profiling causes distrustful, unhappy relationships between certain communities and law enforcement officials. It also wastes police officers' time by keeping them from catching real criminals. For instance, if officers pull over too many black drivers just because of their skin color, they're missing the chance to catch guilty suspects of any color. According to one study, 24 percent of the drivers the police in Missouri pulled over had drugs or other illegal material. Meanwhile, only 19 percent of black drivers did. That means the more black drivers they pulled over, the more likely they were to let guilty white suspects slip away.[5]

Racial profiling also violates the rights guaranteed in the US Constitution. For instance, the Fourth Amendment guarantees "the right of the people to be secure in their persons, houses, papers, and effects, against unreasonable searches and seizures, shall not be violated . . . but upon probable cause . . ." This means citizens should be free from searches unless the government—including police—has reason to suspect them of a crime. The Fifth Amendment states, "No person shall be compelled in any criminal case to be a witness against himself . . . without due process of law . . ." This part of the amendment refers to suspects' rights to remain silent and not incriminate themselves. And the Fourteenth Amendment states "nor shall any State . . . deny to any person within its jurisdiction the equal protection of the laws." This means all American citizens deserve equal treatment under the law.

Suspicions of Muslims after 9/11

The terrorist attacks of September 11, 2001, carried out by the militant Islamic terrorist group Al Qaeda, were deeply shocking to the United States. In an attempt to fight terrorism, the US government has treated its population of six million Muslim citizens with heightened suspicion. Some have been required to register under a special program. The FBI has admitted to spying

What Is Racial Profiling?

After the September 11, 2001, terrorist attacks, the New York Police Department, in conjunction with the CIA, sent undercover officers to monitor Muslim businesses and mosques.

on Muslim neighborhoods, including mosques, and imprisoning up to one thousand Muslim men for long periods of time. These men were later released as innocent with no charges. Muslims also face frequent harassment at airports.

In recent years, the growing threat abroad of the self-proclaimed Islamic State (ISIS) militant group has given the US government an excuse to threaten the civil rights of innocent Muslim Americans. Having their loyalty and patriotism questioned, being pressured to spy, and being undermined makes many members of the Muslim community feel unsafe.

New York City is one of the most diverse cities in the world. It might seem as if it would be as accepting and tolerant a city as one could find. But New York City has interfered with the lives of Muslims in some particularly harsh ways in recent years. Undercover New York Police Department (NYPD) officers spied on Muslims in Arab neighborhoods in New York City, New Jersey, Connecticut, and Pennsylvania to listen in on gossip at cafes, restaurants, and halal butcher shops. They went to mosques, kept track of who went to services, and listened to what was said. They also used a technique they called create and capture. This method involved initiating and recording conversations with Muslims about terrorism or expressing anti-American sentiments to them. These conversations were recorded in hopes that the individuals would give up useful information. What was the end result of create and capture? Zero arrests.

According to a report called "Mapping Muslims: NYPD Spying and its Impacts on American Muslims," innocent Muslims have been traumatized by this post-9/11 spying. For example, when Grace [name has been changed] was sixteen, police officers came to her house while she was alone. They searched through her belongings and her computer. Then they offered her a job as an informant. She later said, "Everyone is being asked to spy, and I know it myself they must have been threatened or bribed to spy. Nobody would just do it voluntarily. And they probably get people in trouble. I know this because they tried to bribe me."[6]

This has led to a feeling of being spied upon all the time and of constant distrust. According to the report, many people don't trust those outside their family circles. As one young man, Faisal Hashmi, said, "I don't want any new friends. If I don't know you and your family, or know that you have a family that I can check you back to, I don't want to know you."[7]

Another young man, Ahsan Sama, said, "Free speech isn't a privilege that Muslims have."[8]

Amira [name has been changed], a Sunday school teacher, said, "Even if we know we have rights, we know that they don't apply equally to everyone."[9]

Latino Americans Under Pressure

Most Latinos who live in the United States are citizens. But as many as twelve million undocumented workers have crossed into the United States, mostly from Mexico, to take low-paying jobs, such as harvesting crops. Because the US government tries to find and deport these workers back to their home countries, this puts pressure on those US citizens who came from Mexico. Because they look and speak like Mexican citizens, they are frequently viewed with suspicion by the Immigration and Naturalization Service (INS) and Border Patrol officers, as well as regular police officers. For example, Tiburcio Briceno, a US citizen who was born in Mexico, was driving a work van in Livonia, Michigan, when he was turned in to US Customs and Border Protection and his van was impounded. Even though he could show a valid chauffeur's license and prove he was a US citizen, no one believed him. The ACLU defended him and helped him retrieve the van.[10]

According to a recent Gallup poll, 25 percent of Hispanics—another term commonly used to refer to US citizens from lands with a Spanish-speaking heritage—felt discriminated against in a single month, May 2015. The most frequent area of life in which they felt

Are You Being Racially Profiled?

In their quest to crack down on illegal immigrants, officials often target all Latinos. US citizens and immigrants who are in the country legally have been detained and harrassed for no lawful reason.

discriminated against was by the police—10 percent. Foreign-born Hispanics report more mistreatment than those born in the United States.[11]

Other groups face discrimination and profiling, as well, including Native Americans, Asians, and Pacific Islanders. People can face discrimination for their skin color, their language, their distinctive dress, or all three. Whatever the reason may be, it's wrong.

3

On the Street

On September 9, 2015, James Blake, an African American professional tennis player who was once ranked fourth in the world, was waiting for a car outside his New York City hotel. Suddenly, a white man in a T-shirt and shorts tackled him to the ground and ordered him to roll over on his face. Soon, Blake was handcuffed and surrounded by what turned out to be five police officers. He was told he had been identified as a suspect in an identity-theft ring. Finally, one of the officers figured out they had the wrong man.

Originally, Blake didn't want to talk about what happened to him. But later, he decided he had to. "I have a voice," Blake said. "But what about someone who doesn't? . . . I was tackled for no reason and that happens to a lot of people who don't have a media outlet to voice that to."[1]

Are You Being Racially Profiled?

Professional tennis player James Blake was unceremoniously and unnecessarily tackled to the ground by a plainclothes police officer who mistook him for a fraud suspect.

After Blake found out that the policeman who jumped on him has been sued four times for using excessive force, Blake called for the cop to lose his job. "In my opinion he doesn't deserve to ever have a badge and a gun again, because he doesn't know how to handle that responsibility effectively," he told *Daily News*. "He doesn't deserve to have the same title as officers who are doing good work and are really helping keep the rest of the city safe."[2]

Stop and Frisk

Unfortunately, James Blake is not the only person of color to be treated with excessive force by law officers with little or no provocation. Nor is he the first person of color to be detained, questioned, or manhandled for reasons that don't seem related to behavior but likely point to the person's accent or skin color.

An analysis by the New York Civil Liberties Union revealed that innocent New Yorkers have been subjected to police stops and street interrogations more than five million times since 2002. This is known as stop and frisk, a police tactic that involves the stopping, interrogation, and search of individuals on the street without a legitimate basis of suspicion. The black and Latino communities are the overwhelming target of these tactics. Almost nine out of ten stopped and frisked New Yorkers have been completely innocent, according to the New York Police Department's own reports.[3]

Jonathan Williams, an African American man in New Jersey, remembers a fateful day during his moody teenage years. "I'd known my best friend Roy since kindergarten. He moved away during high school. I'm walking the mile and a half home, and suddenly think of him, the only friend I had, and I get nostalgic." Williams was cutting down a side street when a policeman stopped beside him. As Williams remembers:

> "Were you just yelling something?" the cop asked.
>
> "No."
>
> "You aren't yelling?"
>
> I've just done my homework. I'm coming home from the library. The cops are screaming at me and I can't believe it. I'm one of like four African Americans in town. They've known me all my life. They're yelling at me for walking down the street.[4]

That was the day Williams learned the police were not his friends and that he could not depend on them to protect him.

It may surprise many to hear that racial profiling isn't confined to urban areas; it can happen in America's most exclusive and liberal institutions. One winter day when he was a freshman at

Are You Being Racially Profiled?

Police tend to be suspicious of young men of color who are wearing baggy clothing. This may not be fair, but it is reality. Think about the way you present yourself in public to avoid any trouble.

Harvard University, Madison Shockley II noticed something odd: a Cambridge police cruiser driving onto campus with its lights flashing. Police rarely entered the college grounds—they usually let Harvard's own security team handle any problems. The car stopped, officers jumped out, and Shockley realized the police were staring at him. They ordered him to take his hands out of his winter coat slowly. A crowd watched while he did. Luckily, he could prove he was a Harvard student. But after he did, he wanted to know why he had been stopped. As he wrote in *Huffington Post*, "Dismissively, they tossed a 'You fit the description' over their shoulder. There had been a report of an assault by a black man in a white coat in the subway station at Harvard Square. Yes, I fit the description. I was a black man."[5]

Something similar happened to the son of *New York Times* columnist Charles M. Blow. His son was stopped at gunpoint when he was a student at Yale University. "There is no way to work your way out—earn your way out—of this sort of crisis," Blow wrote afterward. "All of our boys are bound together."[6]

Staying out of Trouble

As these examples prove, it isn't completely possible to stop being racially profiled, but you can help decrease your odds. Just as so many wise parents and guardians say, don't engage in behavior that will make you a target, and don't get yourself into trouble. This means avoid all illegal behavior. The police are supposed to catch people participating in crimes. Don't set yourself up.

Beyond the obvious, though, you might be surprised at what acts could get you a ticket or misdemeanor charge. The number of local, state, and federal laws on the books about how people should walk, bike, drive, skateboard, throw out their trash, take care of their lawns, and listen to music alone is staggering. You can stay ahead of the game by knowing what those laws are.

How can you find out what the laws are about getting around in your community? Research local pedestrian laws by going to your

Are You Being Racially Profiled?

Following his arrest for breaking into his own home, Harvard University professor Henry Louis Gates Jr. and Cambridge police sargeant James Crowley sat down with President Obama and Vice President Biden to discuss race relations in the United States.

local library, town or city hall, police department, or by checking out their websites. Some common laws include not jaywalking, staying on the sidewalk if there is one, and walking on the left side of the street—against traffic—if there isn't. Other smart advice to follow includes not littering, staying out of parks after closing time, and avoiding places that have no trespassing signs. Also, be aware of places where skateboarding is prohibited and don't skateboard there.

Keep a Low Profile

Former police officer Dale Carson says another way to minimize the impact of racial profiling is to avoid the police's attention as much as possible. How? Carson advises staying away from places where the police are likely to be cruising around. If a police car is driving by, keep doing whatever it is you're doing. If you're walking or jogging, keep moving at the same pace. Don't stick your hands into your pockets or purse. Don't make sudden, unpredictable movements. Don't suddenly take off and run as soon as you spot the police.

If you live in a crowded city neighborhood, stay off the streets as much as you can—especially at night. Why? Urban teens are more likely to spend time outside on the streets because they have less space at home than kids who live in suburban or rural neighborhoods. That makes kids more visible to cops. As Carson says, more visibility makes more danger. Then teens get arrested for minor offenses, such as jaywalking, dancing in the street, or skateboarding. It's not fair, it's not right, but it's better to know than not know.

He also suggests avoiding crime scenes because many criminals like coming back to the scene of their crime. Police sometimes take pictures of people who like to stare at crime scenes. Carson says it's a bad idea to be in those pictures.[7]

Following these guidelines may not stop racial profiling, but they will at least increase your odds of being left alone.

Are You Being Racially Profiled?

If the Police Stop You

When you are out and about, it pays to be street smart and learn how to act around police. With helpful adults or peers, practice learning how to stay calm, respectful, and in control of your words, body language, and emotions. If possible, it's a good idea to get to know your local police officers. If they have a relationship with you and know you are a good citizen, they are less likely to stop you for no reason.

If an officer calls you over or comes up to you, you can ask politely, "Is there some reason you are detaining me, officer?" or "Am I free to go, officer?" If the officer says you are free to go, leave immediately. If not, you will know you are under suspicion and that they intend to detain you. Police can ask you questions, but they may stop you only if they have reason to be suspicious that you have or will commit a crime.

The law requires that an officer judges probable cause to frisk you. If an officer insists on frisking you, don't resist, touch the officer, or make any trouble. You can say, "I do not consent to this search," but don't resist physically.

Watch your hands. Don't put them near your waist. Ask permission to move them. Say as little as possible. Anything you say to a police officer can be used against you in court in ways you can't imagine. If you don't want to talk and they say you are not free to go, you can say, "I would like to remain silent."

If an officer asks if he or she can look in your purse or backpack, politely say something such as, "My mother/teacher/pastor advised me not to consent to searches." If they do it anyway, say again, "I do not consent to this search." They may search your bag anyway. Don't try to stop them. But if you end up in court, your refusal to give consent could help you.

If You Need a Lawyer

To prepare yourself if being racially profiled has gotten you into legal trouble, learn as much as you can about the legal system. There are a many books, organizations, and websites that can help you. One organization that can help you is the American Civil Liberties Union (ACLU.org). Another is the legal book publisher NOLO (NOLO.com), which offers free legal advice on their website. NOLO also has a national database of lawyers.

It can be helpful to have the name and number of a criminal defense attorney just in case of trouble. You can search NOLO or ask for recommendations from people you know. You or your parents may want to talk to a lawyer briefly to see if he or she would be a good fit for you. Attorneys often give brief consultations for free. Then, carry the lawyer's name and phone number with you in your wallet or purse along with:

- A driver's license or other form of ID
- A charged cell phone or camera for recording any kind of problem situation
- Contact numbers of people to call in case of emergency

Another extremely helpful document is the ACLU's Know Your Rights wallet card. This is a foldable wallet-sized guide advising you about your rights and responsibilities in the event that you are stopped by the police, immigration agents, or the FBI. Find it online at aclu.org/know-your-rights-students-wallet-card.

Biking While Black

Riding a bike sounds like a healthy way to get exercise or just a fun way to get around. But in Tampa, Florida, it can be a good way to get a ticket—if you're black. Over the past twelve years, the city of Tampa has given out ten thousand bicycle tickets. Even though they make up less than 25 percent of Tampa's population, African American citizens were issued 80 percent of the tickets, according to an investigation by the *Tampa Bay Times*. Some of the reasons citizens have been issued tickets have been as minor as failing to

Are You Being Racially Profiled?

African Americans biking in Tampa, Florida, found themselves the target of excessive ticketing. This may sound laughable, but the practice has had severe repercussions.

place their hands on the handlebars, having a missing taillight, or wearing baggy clothes.

A bike ticket may not sound like a big deal, but it can have real consequences. Eric Davis received fourteen bike tickets as a teen. He never got any traffic tickets, but the unpaid bike tickets caused his driver's license to be suspended. When Davis was pulled over while driving one day, he was put in jail. "I didn't know it would go to my license," he said.[8]

How can you find out what the biking laws are in your area? Some towns and cities have workshops on knowing the rules of the road. So do local bike clubs. One key thing to remember is to follow the same laws as cars, such as obeying all traffic signals, signs, and pavement markers. Many states also have helmet laws for young people and rules about maintaining a bike. Some other local rules might include:

- Bikers cannot wear a headset.
- A white headlight and red taillight must be used from dusk to dawn.
- A bell or other audible signal—but not a whistle—is required.
- Working brakes are required.
- Bicyclists are required to use hand signals to turn left and right.

4

Racial Profiling in Cars and Planes

When Alex Landau was nineteen, he was pulled over for making an illegal left turn in his hometown of Denver, Colorado. The police patted down both African American Laundau and his white passenger, Addison. Addison had marijuana in his pocket, and the officer cuffed him. But Landau didn't have any drugs; he'd never been in any trouble. As one officer began searching his car, Landau asked politely, "Can I please see a warrant before you continue the search?"

As he tells it, the police grabbed him and started hitting him in the face while his horrified friend demanded they let him go. It got worse: he heard an officer yell that Landau was reaching for a gun. Landau shouted that he wasn't reaching for anything. Then he heard an officer say, "If he doesn't calm down, we're going to have to shoot him." Landau felt a gun next to his head. He said he expected to be shot. Then, he passed out.

"I woke up to a multitude of officers just standing around me laughing," Landau said. "One officer was like, 'Where's that warrant now?'" and called him a racial slur. He reports that forty-five stitches were required to fix the lacerations on his face—never mind his other wounds and bruises.

It wasn't until he finally saw his mother's horrified face that it hit him how bad things were. Raised in a loving home by white parents, Alex had never thought much about race. He thought that "love would conquer" and "skin color didn't really matter." But now, "I was just another black face in the streets, and I was almost another dead black male."[1] You can see a powerful graphic representation of his ordeal with his and his mother's real words

The Department of Justice states that officers may not use race as a basis for making routine spontaneous decisions, such as an ordinary traffic stop, yet blacks are still stopped more often than whites.

through the oral history project *StoryCorps* at storycorps.org/listen/alex-landau-and-patsy-hathaway.

Driving While Black

What happened to Alex happens frequently to young black men all over the country.

One of the most common places people can be profiled is in their cars. A Department of Justice report found that blacks and Latinos were three times more likely to be searched during a during a traffic stop as white drivers were.[2]

Even being well known and well off doesn't prevent racial profiling. Comedian Chris Rock wanted to make the point that even though he is rich and famous, he is not protected from the problems that other African Americans face, such as being pulled over by the police for no reason. In the spring of 2015, he put selfies of himself up on Twitter each time he was stopped by the police for no reason, which added up to three times in seven weeks.

Another famous actor and comedian, Jamie Foxx, recounted having the same problem. He was driving in his Rolls Royce with the top down on a beautiful Los Angeles day when:

> All of a sudden, [a police car gets] behind me.... he turns his lights on and I'm thinking, "It couldn't be me." And I actually move over and say, "Yeah, go get 'em! Go get those guys" and he was like, "It's you—pull it over!" and when he yelled at me, he yelled like I was crazy. He talked to me like I wasn't human.[3]

Although it is frustrating to know that you could be targeted for a police search, you might as well use that information to your advantage.

Racial Profiling in Cars and Planes

Comedian Chris Rock used social media to share his experiences with racial profiling. Even celebrities and professional athletes have been stopped by police while driving simply because of their skin color.

Are You Being Racially Profiled?

1. When you go out driving, always bring the following: your driver's license, pen and paper, a charged cell phone, and a camera if your cell phone doesn't have one. If the police stop you, you will need your driver's license, registration, and proof of insurance. Keep these in an easy-to-reach location, such as on the passenger seat or dashboard.

2. Test the car's lights before taking it out at night. Make sure it has enough gas and that it's working properly.

3. Don't ever bring anything you would regret the cops finding in your car. And don't let your friends bring alcohol, drugs, or anything else that could get you—or your family—in trouble in your vehicle, either. After a night out with your friends, check everywhere, including under the seats, to make sure they haven't left anything behind.

4. Obey the laws. Don't text and drive. Don't speed. Follow the rules of the road. Driving is serious business. Police are on the lookout for erratic behavior by drivers.

The police are entitled to pull over cars for minor malfunctions, such as broken headlights. According to police officer Steve Pomper, many people get tickets for such simple reasons as broken mirrors, lights that are burned out, registration tabs that are expired, wheels that wobble, the carrying of heavy items that aren't secured safely, mufflers that drag, broken lenses, and license plates that are displayed improperly. He says, "Remember this admonition: Don't give the cop a reason to stop you. All the good driving in the world won't help you one bit if your car gives the officer a reason to stop you."[4]

If Police Stop You

So what should you do if you do get pulled over by the police? Stay seated with the door closed, and wait until the officer comes to you. Don't feel as if you have to roll the window down all the way. Greet

Racial Profiling in Cars and Planes

If you are stopped by the police, don't give officers a reason to arrest you. Remain respectful and speak only when a question has been asked of you. This is not the time for a protest.

the officer politely. If he or she asks for ID, hand him or her your driver's license, registration, and proof of insurance. The officer may ask to search your car. In certain cases, your car can be searched without a warrant. To protect yourself later, you can state that you do not consent to a search. If the officer insists on searching anyway, don't argue. Instead, stay calm and remember every detail you can about the incident for later. If the officer is angry or belligerent, your safety should come first. If you're suspected of drunk driving, you will be asked to take a breath alcohol and coordination test. If you fail the tests or refuse to take them, you will be arrested, your driver's license may be suspended, and your car may be taken away. If you are arrested, your car will probably be searched.

Some traffic or other offenses may require you to go to court on a certain day. Read any ticket or letters you get from the court system carefully. Hold onto them. Put the dates on your calendar, and do not miss them. If there is a fine that needs to be paid by a certain day, make sure you pay it unless you decide to take it to court. If you are expected in court, do not miss the date or you can get into serious trouble. If you feel as if you've been racially profiled—or in any case—it's a good idea to remember what happened as clearly as possible. During the incident, try to memorize the officer's name, badge number, and license plate number. Remember as many details as you can in the order they happened. Write down what the officer said, the way he or she acted, what you said, whether or not you consented to a search, exactly where you were stopped, and the reason the officer gave.

Up in the Air

Racial profiling also occurs frequently during air travel, especially after the attacks of September 11, 2001. In May 2015, an Illinois woman, Tahera Ahmad, was on a United Airlines flight. Ahmad is an interfaith chaplain who wears a traditional Muslim *hijab*, or head covering. Ahmad asked the flight attendant for an unopened can of Diet Coke. Instead of honoring her passenger's simple request,

Racial Profiling in Cars and Planes

Tahera Ahmad was humiliated on a flight simply for wearing traditional Muslim dress. Discriminated against by a flight attendant and fellow passengers, Ahmad's experience brings to light the unfair treatment many Muslims suffer at airports.

the flight attendant snapped, "Well I'm sorry I just can't give you an unopened can, so no diet coke [sic] for you." Then she handed the man sitting next to Ahmad an unopened can of beer. Ahmad wanted to know why the woman refused to give her an unopened can when she gave her seatmate one. The attendant said, "We are unauthorized to give unopened cans to people because they may use it as a weapon on the plane."

Ahmad was shocked. She told the flight attendant that she was discriminating against her. In response, the flight attendant grabbed the man's beer can, opened it, and said to Ahmed, "It's so you don't use [his can] as a weapon." Ahmad looked around. She asked people around her if they'd witnessed the attendant's behavior. Then she got another shock. The man sitting in the aisle across from her yelled, "You Muslim, you need to shut… up." Then he added, "Yes you know you would use it as a weapon so shut… up." After the incident, Ahmad posted on Facebook:

> I felt the hate in his voice and his raging eyes. I can't help but cry on this plane because I thought people would defend me and say something. Some people just shook their heads in dismay.[5]

Note what Ahmad did. She used social media to relay what had happened to her, and the post went viral. She stated her feelings, but she did not get aggressive. If she had been aggressive, she could have found herself in trouble and at the mercy of a larger court system. Now the flight attendant is no longer allowed to serve on planes, and the airline has issued an apology to Ahmad. She educated a vast population about the kind of negative attention Muslim citizens face on a daily basis for nothing other than living their lives.

But rude treatment isn't the worst that Muslims—and other passengers—face because of their ethnic backgrounds.

No Fly List

Some people simply aren't allowed to board an airplane on the basis of their racial or ethnic backgrounds because they are on what's called the No Fly List. According to the ACLU, the No Fly List is a "watch list of people the government has designated as known or suspected terrorists and prohibited from flying to and from the United States and over U.S. airspace."[6] Unfortunately, many innocent people have been placed on the list for a wide variety of reasons—because of clerical errors, having names similar to a suspected terrorist, having any kind of criminal record past or present, or expressing controversial views publicly. An outrageously large number have been stopped for belonging to certain ethnic groups, particularly Muslims or Latinos.

Recently, the FBI admitted that it had placed innocent Muslims on the No Fly List simply to punish them for refusing to spy for the US government. However, the government refused to allow them to sue the FBI for damages.[7]

Sometimes, people are given a hard time returning to the US after visiting another country. But under the Fourteenth Amendment to the US Constitution, both citizens and those who hold green cards have a right to return to the US. If this happens to you, the ACLU recommends calling the Overseas Citizen Service and speaking to a duty officer. Tell the officer that you were denied boarding on a flight when trying to return home to the US, that you seek help with repatriation, and that you would like to coordinate your trip home by plane with the government.

The School to Prison Pipeline

It sounds like the plot of a TV comedy show—a nerdy genius causes a small explosion during a science experiment. Sixteen-year-old Kiera Wilmot was an African American honor student at Bartow High School in Bartow, Florida. One day she was curious and brought a science fair experiment to try at school that mixed household cleaners and aluminum foil. It made a tiny explosion. Her classmates laughed. But the school resource officer didn't. He handcuffed Kiera, arrested her, and took her to a juvenile assessment center. She was charged with two felonies and expelled from school.

Kiera got lucky. The ACLU took up her cause, and the charges were dropped. After a year, she got to return to Bartow High and earn her diploma. Now she is a mechanical engineering major at Florida Polytechnic University.[1] But at one point, her future looked bleak. As her lawyer, Larry Hardaway, told *Business Insider* magazine,

> When you have no-tolerance policies ... you get charged with an offense for something minor. ... It starts you down that road of limiting and hindering your life. You do something like what could potentially happen to Kiera, in which she can't get a certain job, or she can't go to college ... and eventually they lose so much hope and they start committing things that do lead to prison.[2]

That might not have happened in the good old days. Once upon a time, minor misbehaviors could land kids a stern lecture or maybe a detention. But now, burping, forgetting part of a school uniform, eye-rolling, tossing a rubber eraser, wearing a hat, or bringing a pair of nail clippers to school can get young people suspended, expelled, or even beaten or arrested.

Even suspending students can do real harm. When students are suspended, they're not supervised. This can lead them to fall behind in their schoolwork and potentially to them dropping out of school. Robert Balfaz, a UCLA researcher, discovered that ninth graders who were suspended once became high school dropouts twice as often as ninth graders who had never been suspended.[3]

Children of color are disproportionately affected by harsh school discipline. A Columbia University study titled *Pushed Out, Overpoliced and Underprotected* analyzed US Department of Education data. On average, it turned out, black girls were suspended six times more often than white girls. Black boys were suspended three times more often than white boys. Even just going to school felt like punishment for many kids. "They got to search you," one girl said about the security systems at her school. "It feels like you're in jail. It's like they treat you like animals, because they think that's where you're going to end up."[4]

Implicit Bias

There are several reasons why this happens. According to a Stanford University study, one factor is that if a black student and a white student misbehave in exactly the same way, the black student will

Are You Being Racially Profiled?

Texas student Ahmed Mohamed was arrested when a teacher mistook his homemade clock for a bomb. Ahmed's family has decided to move to Qatar to escape the discrimination they faced in the United States.

get punished more harshly. Why? Because of an attitude on the part of teachers and administrators called implicit bias. That is a behavior or attitude that people have even if they aren't aware of it or don't want to have it. In the study, teachers were asked to decide on punishments for a record of a misbehaving student. If the student was identified with a stereotypical black name, such as Deshawn, he got a harsh punishment. If he was identified with a stereotypical white one, such as Jake, he got a light one.

Both black and white teachers punished the student identified as white less. One of the study's authors, Jason Okonofua, a Ph.D. candidate at Stanford, wrote, "All teachers, regardless of race, are more likely to think a black child, as compared to a white child, is a troublemaker." He added, "I think that it attests to the pervasiveness of stereotype effect."[5]

Zero Tolerance Policies

On April 20, 1999, at suburban Columbine High School in Colorado, two white boys shot and killed thirteen people. Horrified parents demanded change. After that, many schools around the United States got metal detectors, drug sniffing dogs, mandatory drug testing, and police officers to prevent tragedies such as Columbine from happening again. Administrators instituted zero tolerance policies, which punish students harshly without considering the circumstances. Under these policies, small mistakes can set students back big time and prevent them from obtaining an education.

One example is what happened to Atiya Haynes, who was expelled from her school because she was carrying a pocketknife that was exactly one-fourth of an inch too long. Atiya's grandfather had given her the tiny pocketknife to protect herself, and she left it in her backpack and forgot about it. Her backpack was searched at a football game, and she was suspended for her entire senior year.[6]

Are You Being Racially Profiled?

Whether they are aware of it or not, teachers are statistically more apt to punish students of color over white students. Thus, African American students are more represented in detention halls.

The School to Prison Pipeline

Segregated Second-Class Schools

Another reason students of color are at risk for being put on a path to prison is that the schools they attend are often worse than those white children attend, and the schools have a harsher attitude toward the children who attend them.

Currently, the percentage of African American students attending majority white schools is now at its lowest point in almost fifty years.[7] Why is this a problem? Schools with more black, Latino, and other students of color tend to be located in more impoverished areas. These schools tend to be overcrowded, receive fewer resources, and have fewer staff members to help troubled students. Instead of treating students as individuals who might need help, these overwhelmed schools are more likely to punish anyone who gets out of line. To do that, they employ police as school resource officers who carry guns or Tasers and use drug sniffing dogs to patrol the hallways and look for trouble. Kids are going to school too scared to concentrate on their studies because police are standing in hallways and watching them with suspicion with their hands resting on guns. Situations that would have been handled by school officials with education backgrounds and the students' best interests at heart in the past are now often handled by school resource officers instead. Furthermore, the more time police spend watching any group of individuals, the more likely they are to spot those individuals misbehaving.

At a majority white school, administrators are more apt to talk through problems and see students as individuals who need help. The presence of school resource officers in majority nonwhite schools, on the other hand, leads to an attitude of heightened suspicion and distrustfulness, in which students can end up being suspended or face other harsh punishments. Take the example of Zahrod Jackson, seventeen, who got into a verbal argument with a cafeteria worker in his high school in Middletown, Connecticut. She screamed at him because she thought he was stealing a Jamaican beef patty that he thought came with his lunch, and he felt publicly humiliated. The appropriate solution to such a problem would be to have an administrator take the arguing parties into another room to work it out. Instead, the armed school resource officers rushed over, threw Zahrod on the floor, and—without warning—Tasered him five times, which burned him and caused him intense pain. They did not offer him medical treatment. Instead, he was arrested. Now his mother is suing the school and the officers in federal court.[8]

As well as being beaten, suspended, or expelled, students of color—and those with disabilities—can end up in overcrowded juvenile detention facilities after being accused of misbehavior. That's what happened to an eighth grader from Louisiana who was arrested after allegedly throwing Skittles at another student on a bus. The boy was arrested and handcuffed in front of his class by an officer. When he cried out as the officer twisted his arm, the officer said he was going to also charge him with resisting arrest. The boy was held at a Juvenile Detention Center for six days. His mother was not told where he was. After he was released, he and his mother left the district.[9]

Because many of these detention centers don't have teachers or textbooks, kids can lose valuable learning time. Often, when students want to go back to their regular schools, the schools make it difficult for them to return.

Making School Positive: Staying Out of the Pipeline

Learning to deal with strict school rules can help you gain valuable skills to navigate the adult world more effectively. When you go to work, you'll probably have to deal with rules that you don't like, too—it's just part of life. Here are some points to keep you out of trouble on your educational path.

The School to Prison Pipeline

The school experience for students of color has become increasingly aligned with prison conditions. Students pass through security checks, and armed school resource officers keep the peace.

Are You Being Racially Profiled?

1. **Keep your nose clean.** School officials have the right to search students without a warrant if they believe the student has drugs, weapons, or other illegal substances. They can pat down students, ask them to empty their pockets, and search backpacks and lockers. If they find something illegal, they can call the police.

2. **Follow the rules.** If there is a dress code, don't break it. If you aren't allowed to bring cell phones, don't. Don't get out of your seat without permission.

3. **Keep your cool.** Adults such as teachers and principals have power over you. Practice expressing yourself respectfully even if you disagree with them. Being able to stay polite with powerful people is a useful skill for adult life.

4. **Avoid fights in school.** If you have a disagreement, don't get physical or use racist or sexist language. This is never acceptable and is cause for severe punishment.

5. **Network.** Build up a network of adult allies before you need help. Find teachers and administrators you respect and let them be your mentors. Learn from them, and they will be able to vouch for you if you do get into trouble.

6. **Get your education.** Whatever you do, think of the primary purpose of school: getting your high school diploma. Learn everything you can—you never know when you're going to need it. Learn how the government works, learn about the Constitution, and learn about the Bill of Rights. Whatever you do, don't let anyone cheat you out of your education—now or in the future. Use school for the education you can get out of it—don't let it use you. Don't let it force you out. Read, listen, and absorb everything you can learn.

The School to Prison Pipeline

Developing positive relationships with teachers or school officials can work to your advantage if you ever find yourself in trouble. Having an ally to advocate on your behalf can keep you out of the pipeline.

Responding to Punishment

If you get in trouble, you do not have to talk to the school officials if you think the punishment is unfair. If you are going to talk, insist on getting a parent or other responsible adult to help you.

If you and your guardians are not satisfied by the results of a punishment and feel it is unjust, take it to a higher level. If you reach the highest level without satisfaction, attend a school board meeting and protest. If that doesn't work, tell your story to a local newspaper or put it on social media. Be civil. That may gain you helpful results. If some rules seem truly unreasonable, join an organization or create a petition to try to get them changed.

There are ways to help improve the situation and shift the balance toward a healthier relationship between students and schools so fewer students drop out and more students get a better education. One example is what happened at Richmond High School in California. The school drastically cut its suspensions by setting up a Youth Court, where students act as judges, lawyers, and jurors and decide on consequences for their misbehaving peers. Instead of being kicked out of school and losing class time, these kids stay in school and make up for what they did wrong while knowing that their classmates, who understand what they are going through, have decided the punishment—not law enforcement officials.[10]

Police Overreach?

The police play an important role in public life. They break up fights, keep criminals from breaking into homes, and even deliver babies in a pinch. They keep traffic moving when accidents happen. They have to make on-the-spot decisions about all kinds of complicated problems on a day-to-day basis. They see a variety of tragic and difficult circumstances. One aspect of their job that can be demoralizing is their responsibility to look for problems. When your job is to find the worst in people, it can make you cynical and lead others to see you as a threat. It can be heartbreaking to dedicate your life to public service and be treated like an enemy.

These days, the relationship between police and many citizens is strained, particularly in communities of color. Crime rates are much higher in many African American and Latino communities than in white areas. However, most African Americans who live in high-crime communities do not want more police presence. According to

Are You Being Racially Profiled?

a Gallup poll aggregating data from 2006 to 2014, urban blacks have little confidence in the police. While 57 percent of all Americans said they have "a great deal" or "quite a lot" of confidence in the police, just 34 percent of blacks do. Of those living in urban areas, only 26 percent do.[1]

Some people believe the power of the police has allowed them not just to isolate themselves but also to put themselves above the law, especially in communities of color. There's a dangerous standoff between people of color and the police, and it's causing a mutually uncomfortable and disconnected relationship in which neither party feels respected, understood, or safe. Police can feel alone, isolated, unsupported by friendly faces, easy to spot in their uniforms, and easy to target by hostile attention as they drive around in their police cruisers or walk their beats on lonely streets.

A Difficult Job

Police have to face a lot of hostility. Moses H. is a young man who lives in Bedford-Stuyvesant, a mostly black inner city neighborhood of Brooklyn, New York. Though he shares the frustration that many of his neighbors have with the aggressive tactics he's seen police officers use, he also feels sorry for them. He finds that many of his neighbors feel hostile toward police even if they're arresting someone who might well be guilty of committing a crime against someone who lives in the neighborhood. He says that signs in windows of apartments, businesses, and even churches have antipolice slogans. He said, "One time I saw a policeman walking by on patrol. Across the street a guy cursed at the officer, just out of the blue, for no reason. Then he ran down into the subway before the policeman could see who it was."[2]

Police have been treated disrespectfully in many places around the country. An Arby's restaurant in Pembroke Pines, Florida, refused to serve a police officer just because she was in uniform.[3] There have been antipolice demonstrations in New York City; Madison, Wisconsin; Cleveland, Ohio; and other cities. Retired

Police Overreach?

Every day, police officers enter situations that are extremely dangerous and even life threatening. It is important to understand the tremendous pressure they are under.

officer Anthony Scaglione, who spent twenty-one years working in the Ithaca, New York, police department, asked, "When did we become the bad guys? It's heartbreaking what's happening, the disrespect we're receiving these days."[4]

Armed to the Teeth?

Some say the police have become way too powerful in recent years and that they have lost, in many cases, the sense of mission they need—that they are supposed to keep the peace but instead they are almost like warriors in hostile territory.

How did this happen? One cause is the War on Drugs, a massive campaign to end the illegal drug trade, started by President Richard Nixon in the 1970s. Another is the attack on the World Trade Center on September 11, 2001. After 9/11, the federal government gave thousands of pieces of leftover military equipment to police departments all over the United States to fight the War on Terror and War on Drugs. Some of the equipment they've given—even to small town police departments—includes grenade launchers, military-grade body armor, M-16 rifles, night-vision goggles, .50 caliber machine guns, and mine-resistant armored personnel carriers, helicopters, and tanks.[5]

All of this equipment, and new laws allowing the police more freedom to intrude upon citizens' rights as they go after suspects, has made law enforcement officers more powerful. But has it made them more effective? That is an open question.

The government's hope was that this equipment would help police around the country be more effective at their jobs. It has certainly made the police a more powerful presence. But there is a drawback to giving police all of this armor. It can lead to the appearance, at least, that some police departments have taken an attitude of "if you have a hammer, everything feels like a nail" toward policing—that is, if you have the equipment, it's going to feel as if you need it.

Police Overreach?

Many local police departments have been equipped with military-grade gear that is not necessary for most situations. This adds to the public perception that police are all too ready to use it.

One sign of how militarized some police departments have recently become is the increase in the use of Special Weapons and Tactics (SWAT) teams. According to police expert Radley Balko, during the 1970s there were about three hundred SWAT raids per year; as of 2005, there were forty thousand per year.[6] These highly trained and armed units have taken over tasks that used to be done by regularly uniformed police officers, including carrying out search warrants and raids for minor drug charges or gambling. These raids disproportionately target blacks and Latinos. This has affected the ways police departments view themselves. They recruit new officers with video clips of SWAT teams storming into homes with smoke grenades and firing automatic weapons.

An example of this hyper-militarization occurred at 5:30AM on August 20, 2014, when a SWAT team burst into a Worcester, Massachusetts, apartment with their guns out. They wanted to arrest a suspected drug dealer. Instead, they came upon a sleeping family—Bryant Alenquin, Marianne Diaz, and their two children. They handcuffed the father, trained their guns on the mother and children, and carried out their search. Their lawyer later said, "You can imagine 10 officers looking and pointing guns at a… 23-year-old mother protecting her two kids."[7] To make things worse, the suspect the police were looking for was already in police custody.

As frightening as their experience was, Diaz and Alenquin were lucky. Sometimes, the results can be tragic. According to the ACLU, "heavily armed SWAT teams are raiding people's homes in the middle of the night, often just to search for drugs," which causes people to die needlessly during the raids.[8]

The Danger of Fearful Police

Recently, some police unions and other activists have expressed concern that there is a war on cops. They point to citizen groups that have protested against police. That puts pressure on officers and makes them feel harassed. Some police shows on TV make it look as if police officers are constantly getting into gun battles with

Police Overreach?

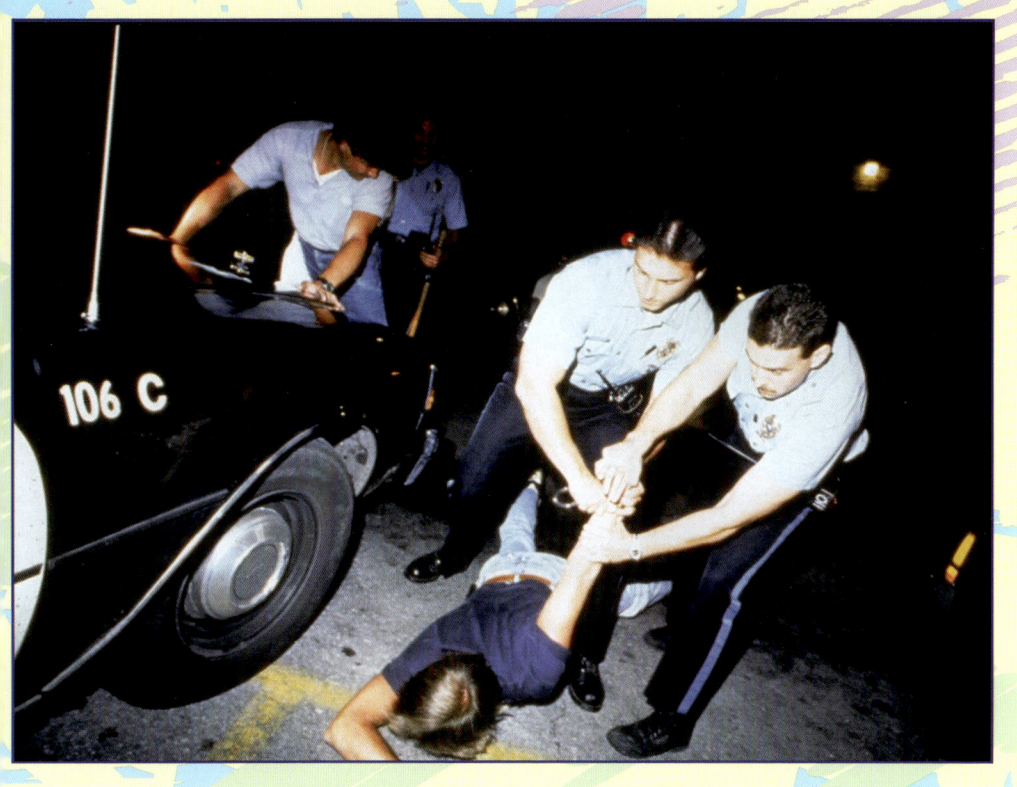

TV cop dramas give the false impression that every police interaction is a dramatic arrest or shoot-out. The truth is, the majority of situations that police encounter can be solved with a respectful conversation.

criminals. Of course, anything can happen on the job. But statistically speaking, being a police officer is safer than it has ever been.

According to Balko, in terms of rate of police deaths, 2013 was the safest year for police in more than a century. Around the entire United States, thirty-one police officers died of gunshot wounds. The problem is, Balko said, if police are told constantly their jobs are dangerous, they are not only likely to be more frightened and stressed as they do their job, but they are also more likely to be a danger to the citizens they are supposed to protect. "A cop who is constantly told that his job is dangerous and that every interaction with a citizen could be his last will naturally be more likely to reach for his weapon when it isn't necessary," Balko wrote in *The Washington Post*.[9]

When police become so resistant to facing danger that they prioritize their own safety over that of unarmed citizens they are sworn to protect, they become a danger to those citizens. Of course, it is important for police to be safe. But many experts argue that a certain amount of risk comes with the job. "Police officers' first responsibility is not to protect themselves at any cost but to run certain risks in order to keep citizens safe while protecting their rights. . . . police cannot armor . . . themselves in a way that hurts their primary objective: catching criminals and protecting civil liberties," said Daniel Bier, of the Foundation for Economic Education.[10]

Military expert William Lind agrees. "Cops' mission is to keep us safe, if necessary at risk to themselves," he wrote in *The American Conservative*. He believes that when police wear riot gear and carry military-grade equipment, they send the wrong message. He says the police's primary job is to prevent crimes, not to catch criminals afterward, and that to prevent crimes, police need to talk to citizens. If police are too intimidating, he says, people will not get close to them. "Citizens are comfortable talking to police who are 'Officer Friendly,' the nice-guy cop on the beat whose uniform, equipment, and demeanor are unthreatening," he wrote in *The American*

Conservative. "Few people like shooting the breeze with one of Darth Vader's storm troopers."[11]

The Thin Blue Line

Police departments have guidelines about the appropriate use of escalating force. But generally speaking, police are given a lot of latitude to determine what self-defense means. When officers feel threatened or need to protect others, they are allowed to protect lives with their guns. However, such large numbers of citizens die at the hands of police officers each year that many are skeptical of the need for such deadly force. *The Guardian* newspaper collects data about these deaths in its project called *The Counted*. As of October 8, 2015, 891 people had been killed in the United States by police officers for that year alone. Of those, 461 were white, 217 were black, and 130 were Hispanic or Latino.[12]

The police have killed thousands of people since 2005, according to *The Washington Post*. For those deaths, fifty-four officers have been charged. So far, only eleven have been convicted. Jurors usually see the officer as "the good party in the fight," said David Harris, a University of Pittsburgh law professor and expert in police use of force. "To get them to buy into a story where the officer is the bad guy goes fundamentally against everything they believe."[13]

As former Baltimore policeman Michael Woods told *Slate*, "What [people] fear is that [police] can get away with whatever we choose to get away with....The laws are to the point where anybody can be locked up pretty much for any time..... So you're constantly ready to be a problem."[14]

Furthermore, good cops face intense pressure to cover for bad cops. Most members of the police believe there must never be a break in the thin blue line—a term that stands for police as the protection between citizens and the criminal element. But some police officers will stick up for one another no matter what. When a police officer points out the misbehavior of another officer, he or she can be ostracized or face retribution. Clatskanie, Oregon, police

Are You Being Racially Profiled?

Instead of fostering a contentious relationship between the police and citizens, the focus should be on improving community interactions. This includes getting to know your local police so that you can build a mutual sense of respect.

officer Alex Stone was horrified when he saw Chief Marvin Hoover comparing an African American woman to a monkey, "making loud monkey sounds . . . [and] scratching and chanting." So he filed an official complaint.

But Stone was told that if he spoke out against a fellow officer, the city and the chief would "make his life hell."

Afterward, "There was a nail in my tire," he said. He was forced off the road while he was out driving with his wife. He even received death threats via email. He told *The Oregonian* that city officials remained unhelpful. "Not one person will speak to me," he said. "It's insane."[15]

A Better Relationship?

So how can citizens and police have a more productive relationship? Consider the following:

Accountability: Some experts say it should be easier to get rid of bad cops. If bad cops were held accountable for their actions, good officers would not be dragged down by the pressure to ignore, or worse, stand behind the behavior of their badly behaved peers.

Take away the armor: Rethink the idea that more equipment is better. Have police officers dress in normal uniforms and interact with citizens face-to-face—not from behind a riot shield or a submachine gun.

Mutual respect: Police and citizens need to find ways to meet with each other and share their common goals and values for the community. It's fair to protest bad policies. But being openly hostile to a police officer who is just walking down the street doing his or her job is not just unproductive, it's nasty. Remember: There really are hero cops, too.

7

Juvenile Injustice

Kalief Browder was fifteen when he was arrested for stealing a backpack. Despite claiming his innocence, he was put in jail in New York City's infamous Rikers Island jail complex. Because his family could not afford to pay his bail, Kalief was held for three years while waiting for a trial. Angry that he wouldn't confess, guards tortured him by placing him in solitary confinement for more than eight hundred days. They beat him. They allowed other prisoners to beat him, too. Even though his accuser had left the country and no trial was possible, Kalief remained in jail. He tried to kill himself several times while in jail, but he didn't succeed. Finally, prosecutors gave up and released him.

Kalief refused to get a criminal record for a crime he did not commit. After he got out of jail, he spoke out publicly so others could be helped. He started going to college, where he was a popular young man and had a 3.5 grade point average. But Kalief's story does not have a happy ending. The nightmarish experience at Rikers Island haunted him. It changed him. In 2015, after telling his mother he couldn't take it anymore, Kalief Browder hung himself.[1]

There are many different ways young people can slip through the cracks—their cries unheard and their vulnerability unprotected. Unless they have an advocate, all kinds of abuses are possible. The playing field is not even.

The Purpose of Juvenile Justice

When a young person commits a crime, many times he or she may need to learn a lesson. But what is the purpose of the lesson? Experts say the person is supposed to come out of the experience learning how to be better. Ideally, that person should learn right from wrong and that doing bad things will bring undesirable results. Time spent in juvenile detention should be thought of as a kind of time out that will let the person rethink his or her bad behavior and learn individual responsibility. Unfortunately, it doesn't always work that way.

Critics of the court system argue that it naturally allows many things to stand in the way of juvenile justice. One aspect of the court system that outsiders might not be aware of is that lawyers, judges, and other members of the court aren't necessarily looking for the truth. They are working in an adversarial system. That is, they are arguing the strongest case they can for their side while hoping to get the best deal they can. Justice can be left behind in the process.

The Cash Bail Problem

One problem that defendants, both young suspects such as Kalief Browder and adult ones, can face is the cash bail system. In many places, when a person is arrested, they can be put into jail until their trial. But they can leave if they pay bail, or money that the court system holds onto to make sure the defendant will have a reason to show up to trial. In many places, the amount of bail is too high for poor people to pay or even borrow.

Are You Being Racially Profiled?

Mourners placed flowers atop photographs of Kalief Browder, the young man who committed suicide after being detained at Rikers Island for three years without having been convicted of a crime.

Juvenile Injustice

That means if the price of bail doesn't take into account people's finances, it is unfair. That's because people end up stuck in jail for weeks or months and end up making deals to get out in exchange for time served. Bail is one of the most important decisions that can be made about a case because once young people have a conviction on their record, it can be a lifelong problem. This system encourages defendants to make deals and plead guilty to a smaller crime just to get out of jail—even if they aren't guilty. Why would anyone plead guilty to a crime they haven't committed? Because they may feel hopeless of ever getting justice or because they have other responsibilities to get back to.

Time in detention can be deeply harmful to young people. According to Robert L. Listenbee, the administrator of the Office of Juvenile Justice and Delinquency Prevention, "Research has … shown that the minute a youth sets foot in detention or lockup, he or she has a 50 percent chance of entering the criminal justice system as an adult."[2]

The Teenage Brain

The teenage brain is wired differently than adult brains. Scientific research has shown that our brains—particularly those parts involved in decision-making—don't fully develop until around age twenty-five. Teens are more impulsive. But they may also be more resilient. Sometimes teens who are troublemakers grow up to be perfectly decent human beings. Risk taking is part of youthful behavior.

Criminalizing silly pranks and youthful experiments can be especially damaging. It inhibits normal development. Kenneth King, Associate Justice Massachusetts Juvenile Court at Massachusetts Trial Court, wrote that "[e]ven if an adolescent has an 'adult-like' capacity to make decisions, the adolescent's sense of time . . . emotions, and vulnerability to pressure will often drive him or her to make very different decisions than an adult would in similar circumstances."[3]

Teenagers are not given the full rights of adulthood yet. Adults are supposed to look out for their interests. Instead, there are people who just act as adversaries and push them through the system. In some places, there are few legal defenders to look after them.

Status Offenses

Many young people are forced into juvenile detention because of an unfair loophole in the law. People who are under eighteen can be charged with status offenses. This is a category of offenses that are only offenses because of the status of the person who commits them. Some status offenses that those under the age of eighteen can commit are truancy or skipping school, buying cigarettes, and breaking curfew. These offenses can get kids into a lot more hot water than they think. And they may not know how much until it's too late because unlike adults, they may not know—or in some cases might not even have—their right to legal representation, or a lawyer, that adults would get to help them navigate their way through the courts. Why? Because technically, status offenses aren't crimes. Youth who become involved in the juvenile justice system are often denied procedural protections, such as representation by a lawyer.

In places as far apart as Tennessee and Washington state, kids who skipped school because they were bullied have ended up in handcuffs, torn away from their families, and locked up in juvenile prisons. Many times, young people get unfavorable police records, as well. Patricia Puritz, executive director of the nonprofit National Juvenile Defender Center in Washington, DC, says there's a big problem across the United States in trying to make sure that children get the legal help they need when they have to appear in court for status offenses, misdemeanors, or crimes. She says, "Little people, little justice."[4]

How to Protect Yourself

How can you avoid this happening to you if you get into legal trouble? If at all possible, get a criminal defense lawyer. If your family cannot

Juvenile Injustice

You might be surprised by the minor offenses that can land teens in juvenile detention. One is skipping school. Such a seemingly harmless action can snowball into a serious consequence. It is important to understand your rights as a juvenile.

afford a lawyer, ask about court appointed lawyers. But be aware that many court appointed lawyers have large caseloads and cope with them by making deals. If you are innocent—or even if you have done wrong but are serious about wanting to make amends—think carefully before agreeing to a deal. Be aware that you have rights. Don't be tricked into taking a plea deal that gives you a criminal record if you can possibly avoid it. It is much better to do community service, pay a fine, or make almost any other accommodation than to have a negative mark on your record.

Sometimes there are reasons to put off a court date. One of the most important is that you don't want to go into court without a copy of the police report and any evidence that the police have against you. Remember, most police cruisers now have cameras. You will want the full report and the video evidence before trial. You will also want to gather all the evidence you can about your innocence, such as any witnesses that might testify on your behalf.

When you go to court, dress formally and respectfully. Court is a serious and intimidating place. Behave with your best manners. If you are willing to make a deal, show remorse and why you would not repeat the action. Find out if you can pay a fine or do community service rather than jail time if you have done something wrong.

If you are taken into police custody, there may be a prosecutor who can dismiss the case, handle it informally, or file formal charges. Some factors the prosecutor may consider are your age, the severity of the crime, the evidence against you if there is any, and your family and its influence on you.

If the case is handled informally, no charge will be filed against you. However, you may appear before a judge and could face certain consequences, such as getting counseling, paying a fine, performing community service, or getting probation.

If you get probation, you will be required to have meetings with a probation officer for a certain period, such as six months or a year. The probation officer will set the meeting times. It is extremely important to show up early. Dress nicely and have a good attitude.

Juvenile Injustice

If you find yourself in court, know how to conduct yourself properly. Dress in conservative attire. Speak respectfully to the judge. Prove that you understand and regret your mistakes.

Be prepared for drug testing and to show ways you are making efforts to improve your life, such as getting an after-school job or going to self-help groups. Missing meetings with a probation officer can result in harsh consequences, such as being sent to formal court.

If a young person is charged, or arraigned, in front of a juvenile court, the judge will make a ruling based on the seriousness of the offense and the young person's efforts at self-improvement. Some of the options judges have include requiring counseling, reimbursing a victim, obeying curfews, or even placing the student in a juvenile detention home. If the offense is serious enough, the student may be charged as an adult, which can result in harsher sentencing.

Are You Being Racially Profiled?

A restorative justice teacher speaks with students from Ralph Bunche High School in Oakland, California. Restorative justice programs, which place the focus on taking responsibility and making amends, are increasingly used in schools.

Judges do have some leeway, so be sure to present your most positive side. Think of any contributions you make to the community or any mitigating factors that contributed to the trouble you're now in. If you get community service, make sure you never miss a commitment, and don't have a bad attitude about doing the work. Minor infractions often mean kids get in more serious trouble.

Expunging a Record

If you are convicted of a crime, your record might be sealed if you are a minor. That means you would no longer have to answer yes to the question "Have you ever been convicted of a crime?" after you have served your sentence. However, if it is not sealed, you may be able to get it expunged, or removed, after you turn eighteen. You may have to go to court and pay a fine to get it removed. Whatever it costs in terms of inconvenience, time, or money, do it. Having a clean record is one of the best investments you could make.

Restorative Justice

Sometimes, kids aren't perfect, and they do get into trouble. But that doesn't mean a juvenile detention center is always the best solution. Some places have restorative justice programs. In these programs, kids who wrong others or commit violations sit down with those they hurt and supporters for both sides. Both parties come up with a plan so the young man or woman can do something to make up for the harm they did to the victim, community, his or her own family, and, most importantly, his- or herself. Oakland, California, has a restorative justice program. Facilitator Sujatha Baliga says that restorative justice works because in her opinion, "Getting formally processed through the juvenile justice system does nothing to fight crime. If anything it does more to increase crime."[5]

8

Prisons

Since the 1970s, the prison population in the United States has grown astronomically. Forty years ago, when the United States was in the middle of a crime wave, 300,000 people were in prison. Now crime is way down. But more than 2.3 million people are incarcerated—one out of every hundred people. The United States is home to 25 percent of the prisoners on the entire planet even though it is home to only 5 percent of the world's people.[1]

The Prison-Industrial Complex

So why has the number of people in jails and prisons quadrupled when the crime rate has plummeted? Experts call this growth in prison population the Prison-Industrial Complex. That term is a shorthand way of saying that there is a web of business and political interests that profit from prisons. The increase in prisons has led to a vast increase in the infrastructure of the judicial system. More people are hired to work as guards, cooks, law clerks, and in other aspects of taking care of this huge prisoner population. And these days, many prisons are run not by the government but by private companies out to make a profit.

Today, there are more than one hundred thirty privately owned prisons in the United States. The companies that own these prisons make contracts with states and the federal government that include occupancy requirements. These requirements force the government to keep the prisons anywhere from 80 to 100 percent full even if the crime rate goes down. In Arizona, three private prisons operate with a 100 percent occupancy guarantee. Then the companies use some of that money to support politicians who will vote for laws that

Thanks to laws that are tougher on criminals, rates of incarceration have skyrocketed and prisons have become overcrowded. This has affected the physical and mental health of prisoners.

Are You Being Racially Profiled?

In 1971, President Richard Nixon declared a War on Drugs. On the surface, this seemed like a policy no one could argue with, but it has had disastrous effects on the lives of African American men.

keep people in prison as long as possible. The politicians support them, and the companies build more prisons. Thanks to the Prison-Industrial Complex, the number of inmates in private federal prisons more than doubled between 2000 and 2010.[2]

War on Drugs

A second reason for the high number of prisoners is the War on Drugs. When President Richard Nixon declared the War on Drugs in 1971, the federal government started handing out harsher penalties for possessing or selling drugs. That put a lot of people into prison for a long time.

One effect of the War on Drugs is a disproportionately large number of prisoners of color. Ohio State University professor Michelle Alexander discovered that the government is sending young men of color into prisons in outrageously large numbers. In her book *The New Jim Crow*, she asserts that this high rate of putting black Americans into prisons for small crimes amounts to racism.[3]

According to *The New Jim Crow*, the War on Drugs is the main problem. Since 1970, more and more people have been arrested for selling drugs. These laws disproportionately affect people of color. Approximately 70 percent of drug users are white, 15 percent are black, and 8 percent are Latino. But the Department of Justice reports that among those imprisoned on drug charges, 26 percent are white, 45 percent are black, and 21 percent are Latino.[4]

Harsher Penalties

The penalties for possessing or selling drugs have also become harsher, especially during the crack epidemic in the 1980s. These laws disproportionately affect people of color, as well. In the 1980s, mandatory minimum laws came into being. These laws removed the ability of judges to consider outside factors in sentencing and forced them to give defendants the strongest possible penalties.

In essence, prosecutors, not judges, are determining the sentences. About 95 percent of prosecutors are white, and since they convict 86 percent of the prison population, a nearly all-white group of lawyers is putting a disproportionately black group of defendants in prison. Many of these convictions result from plea bargains, which means these defendants are convicted without a trial. And a recent study found that black men are 65 percent more likely to be charged with crimes carrying a mandatory minimum sentence than the average defendant.[5]

Another cruel law was the three-strikes law. These meant people could get long sentences—even life sentences—if they were convicted of a third crime no matter how much time had passed since the first two. That rule applied even if the third crime was minor, such as shoplifting or having a small amount of marijuana. Twenty-five states passed these laws. California's law, which was amended in 2012, was so harsh that a person who shoplifted could get a longer sentence than someone who committed a murder.[6]

For example, Santos Reyes committed burglary as a juvenile—with no jury trial—which was strike one. The second strike was a robbery that didn't involve injury to anybody. After ten years had passed without incident, Reyes was convicted of perjury, or lying, for submitting a false application while under oath and, as a result of the three-strikes law, he was sentenced to twenty-six years to life.[7]

A similar case is that of Curtis Wilkerson. He stole a pair of socks worth $2.50 in 1995, and for that, he was sentenced to life in prison! Such a crime is usually counted as a misdemeanor, but a prosecutor in Los Angeles got it classified as a felony. Since Wilkerson had already been convicted of abetting two robberies in 1981, when he was nineteen, his petty theft was counted as the third strike, and he received a life sentence.[8]

In California, the social costs of the three-strikes law are borne disproportionately by African American men, who constitute only about 3 percent of the state's population but represent approximately 33 percent of second-strikers and 44 percent of third-strikers among California prison inmates.[9]

Prisons

Under the Three Strikes Law, Gregory Taylor was sentenced to life for breaking into a soup kitchen to steal food. The law is responsible for crowding prisons with minor offenders.

What makes these laws even worse, according to Michelle Alexander, is that they affect 4.8 million others on probation or parole—mostly for nonviolent offenses. She is also concerned about prisoners who have completed their sentences. "This system depends on the prison label, not just prison time," she said. As she points out, after prisoners are released, the punishment does not end. Once they answer yes to a question such as "Have you ever been convicted of a crime?" on an application, it can be difficult for them to obtain a job. They are also denied a number of government services that poor people rely on to get back on their feet when faced with hard times, including public housing, food stamps, educational loans, and other opportunities. They can be automatically denied the chance to serve on juries. In eleven states, people who have served prison sentences are denied the right to vote for the rest of their lives. This disproportionately affects black voting patterns and has the possibility of changing the results of elections. It also destabilizes the entire black community by destroying families, opportunities, and neighborhoods.

All this imprisonment of black adults is taking a toll on black children. Incredibly, a black child today is less likely to be raised by both parents than a black child who was born during slavery. Young people are affected by the fact that too many of their parents are in prison. One example is Jasmine Barclay, who spent much of her life in foster homes because her mother was in jail.

> My mother was arrested when I was about a year old, and it took 18 years before I could have a relationship with her. My father has been in and out of prison, too, and as a result through much of my life I've basically been an orphan . . . even though I've known exactly who should have raised me. America incarcerates more people than any other country, and what people don't understand is that this has consequences for more than the people locked up.[10]

Can Things Change?

The balance is beginning to shift. President Barack Obama has called the War on Drugs a failure. It has been costly. According to the Drug Policy Alliance, enforcing the War on Drugs costs the United States $51 billion each year. As of 2012, the United States had spent about $1 trillion on antidrug efforts.[11]

In the summer of 2015, President Obama commuted the sentences of ninety prisoners, most of whom had been imprisoned under mandatory minimum or three-strikes laws. In the same year, Obama became the first US President to visit a federal prison. He wanted to make a point that prisons need to change. But he wasn't alone. Both Republican and Democratic lawmakers are beginning to want change. Texas Republican Governor Rick Perry was one of the more aggressive prison reformers in the country. In 2011, the state actually closed a prison because it couldn't be filled thanks in large part to the declining incarceration rate. Before Perry, Governor George W. Bush oversaw the construction of thirty-eight new prisons. In 2014, Perry said, "You want to talk about real conservative governance? Shut prisons down. Save that money."[12]

Mass incarceration has massively strained the criminal justice system and led to a lot of overcrowding in US prisons—to the point that some states, such as California, have rolled back penalties for nonviolent drug users and sellers with the explicit goal of reducing their incarcerated population.

In July 2015, the Supreme Court reviewed a three-strikes case involving a white supremacist whose third strike was possessing an illegal firearm. The court wondered if merely possessing a gun was enough to force a person into prison for a lifetime. The court decided no. The landmark decision means that twenty-five states will most likely have to rewrite their three-strikes laws.

But there is a lot more to be done. You can help work to raise awareness for some of the problems in the current justice system—ending the unwinnable War on Drugs, ending mandatory minimum sentences, ending the cash bail system, shutting down private

Are You Being Racially Profiled?

On July 16, 2015, Barack Obama became the first US president to visit a federal prison when he spoke with a small group of inmates at the El Reno prison outside Oklahoma City, Oklahoma.

prisons, restoring ex-offenders' rights to vote, and supporting post-prison programs—because the inflated incarceration rates of black and Latino people has led to their longtime economic and political disenfranchisement.

Many groups are working toward prison reform. You can support organizations such as the American Civil Liberties Union, the Equal Justice Initiative, the Pew Center on the States Public Safety Project, Nation Inside, and Families Against Mandatory Minimums.

9

Fighting Against Racial Profiling

Racial profiling doesn't just affect kids of color. It affects those who care about them. Jane [name has been changed], a white girl from a New Jersey suburb, was driving with her black boyfriend, Mike [name has been changed], in her parents' car one evening when a police car headed in the opposite direction turned around and stopped her. Jane hadn't been driving long, so she was worried she had done something wrong. Her heart was beating fast. But when the officer knocked on the window and asked for her boyfriend's identification, as well as her own, she was puzzled. After all, Mike wasn't the one driving. And the officer had known both kids all their lives—they'd both grown up in the town. Jane remembers the night she realized the privileges she enjoys just because of her skin color.

"Are you all right?" [the officer] asked me, shining the light in both of our faces.

"Yes, officer," I said, wondering what was going on.

"You're sure you're all right?"

"Yes, sir."

"What was THAT about?" I asked [Mike] as I started up the car when he left. And then Mike told me about how police stopped him when he was just walking sometimes. For no reason.

I got it. I didn't want to believe it could really happen. I was so naïve.[1]

As this incident illustrates, everyone is impacted by racial profiling and has a stake in fighting it and the racism that lies behind it. Whites and blacks no longer live completely segregated lives but are interconnected in a variety of ways. This generation may be the most diverse, united generation ever. As depressing as it has been to hear of recent news stories chronicling racial profiling incidents, it has also been helpful in some ways. More Americans of all races are becoming aware of the problems that African Americans and other people of color face. More are connecting the dots and realizing how systemic the problems are. People are developing new strategies and ways to spread ideas. Along with a great sense of sadness, many people feel a sense of determination that seems to have started a process of real change. Large protests in Ferguson, Missouri; Baltimore, Maryland; and other places have started to bring serious attention to the problem—and to embarrass those who have let the wrongs fester for all these years.

It is the struggle of this generation. Perhaps one hopeful element is that it involves young people of all colors working together. Many people look back to the Civil Rights Movement of the 1960s as an

Fighting Against Racial Profiling

Many people, such as those involved in the Black Lives Matter movement, are speaking out against discrimatory practices in the hopes of enacting change in the United States.

exciting time when momentous changes were made. Today, writer Shaun King tweeted, "If you ever wondered what it would be like to live in the Civil Rights Movement, and what role you would play, you are in it right now."[2]

Being an Ally

Whether you've been racially profiled or not, you can help to stop the practice. Whether you have been part of the problem or not, you can still be part of the solution. And you can get to know people of different backgrounds and find sincere people of good faith to be your allies.

One positive factor about today's young people is that they may be the least racist generation in America's history thanks to the gains of the Civil Rights Movement. Students of all races and ethnicities generally believe in equality. Many would be likely to take positive steps to help end racial profiling if they knew what was happening to their black, Hispanic, Islamic, Native American, and other friends who face this form of harassment. Because racial profiling is an issue that affects them or their friends so directly, young people of all races have a motivation and an important stake in the fight against it.

But more needs to be done to bring awareness to this problem. What can young people do, individually or together, to help?

Educate Yourself and Others

Learn more about the scope of this problem. Michelle Alexander's *The New Jim Crow*, which deals with the Prison-Industrial Complex, is an excellent place to start. *Waking up White: And Finding Myself in the Story of Race* by Debby Irving is a first-person narrative from the perspective of a white woman struggling to understand racism, bias, and stereotypes. And many of the websites and other books mentioned in the back section of this resource can help, as well.

If you have been racially profiled, you can use that experience to help others understand. All the feelings that it brings up—from anger to helplessness to shame—can be used to empower positive action. Even if you have merely witnessed racial profiling or have done research to find real-life examples and statistics that show the scope of the problem, there are ways to get your message across.

According to a study by the University of Chicago, virtually all teens have access to the Internet and get news from it. Smart phones are giving individuals even more power. Furthermore, large numbers of young people of all races and ethnicities are using social media platforms, such as Twitter and Facebook, for participatory politics—acts such as starting a political group online, circulating a blog about a political issue, or sending political videos to friends.[3]

Today's tech savvy kids are finding new ways to change the world and connect with each other. Whether it's posting anti-racial-profiling events on Facebook, making a YouTube video or SnapChat, or live tweeting a racial profiling that they're witnessing, this generation of youth is one step—if not more—ahead of adults. "Social media's significance is that it is recognizing different incidents that might have gone unnoticed and sewing them together as a coherent whole," says Ethan Zuckerman, the director of the MIT Center for Civic Media and the author of *Rewire: Digital Cosmopolitans in the Age of Connection*.[4]

Kwame Rose, a twenty-one-year-old civil rights protester from Baltimore, agrees: "Social media plays a big part in everything. I find out information, I put it on Twitter, it starts trending the more people talk about it and then the institutions start feeling the pressure."[5]

An important example of the power of social media is the birth of the Black Lives Matter movement. It all started in July 2013 when Alicia Garza, sitting in a bar in Oakland, California, checked Facebook on her phone and saw the announcement of the not guilty verdict in the trial of George Zimmerman, a neighborhood watch volunteer in Florida who had killed a seventeen-year-old African American boy, Trayvon Martin, the previous year. In the bar, Garza said, "Everything went quiet... And then people started to leave en masse... It was like we couldn't look at each other... It was a verdict that said: black people are not safe in America."

Later, Garza wrote on her Facebook page, "Black people. I love you. I love us. Our lives matter." Garza's close friend, Patrisse Cullors, shared Garza's post with others using the hashtag #blacklivesmatter, and from there, a nationwide social movement was born that has gone on to influence the platforms of presidential candidates and the fight for other issues, such as income inequality.[6]

Twitter, in particular, has been used effectively as a tool to publicize the perspectives of average people on the street. During

Are You Being Racially Profiled?

Following the acquittal of shooter George Zimmerman, crowds took to the streets seeking justice for slain teen Trayvon Martin, who was deemed suspicious for wearing a hood and having dark skin.

protests in Ferguson, Missouri, for the police shooting of unarmed black teenager Michael Brown, and the Freddie Gray protests in Baltimore, demonstrators tweeted what they were seeing, which often contradicted what was being reported by the police or the mainstream media.

And black youth use social networking sites at an even higher rate than white youth. In Todd Wolfson's *Digital Rebellion: The Birth of the Cyber Left*, the author points to the use of social media in grassroots uprisings, such as the Arab Spring, a wave of protests and civil uprisings in the Arab world, and the social and economic movement Occupy Wall Street. "The Cyber Left is about flattening hierarchies, flattening governance processes, combined with using the logic of social networks for deep consensus building," says Wolfson.[7]

You Have the Power to Change the World

Thanks to the connectivity of social media, everyone can be a witness, everyone can become aware about and educate him- or herself about the issues, and everyone can help make sure that the government is held accountable for protecting the rights of its most vulnerable citizens. You can be the eyes and ears of your generation. By tweeting, recording, reporting, and sharing your voice, you can make the world listen.

You can do what Brandon Brooks did. A white fifteen-year-old, Brooks used his cell phone to record racial profiling by police at a now infamous June 2015 incident in McKinney, Texas. After police had been called when a white woman started an argument at a crowded pool party, an emotional policeman began barking out confusing orders to black teens. Then, in what became a shocking viral video, the beefy cop grabbed the braids of a slender African American girl in a bathing suit, flung her to the ground, and kneeled on her back while she screamed. The sight of the large white man suddenly grabbing and kneeling over the small fifteen-year-old was disturbing to many viewers.[8]

Are You Being Racially Profiled?

Demonstrators gathered near a community pool in 2015 to protest the police brutality demonstrated at a McKinney, Texas, pool party. If you feel strongly about racial profiling, make your voice heard.

There are a number of ways you can raise awareness about the issue of racial profiling in your school, as well. There is power in numbers, so find group support. Start an antiracism club. Make a Twitter feed for your club. And remember to add new information to it on a regular basis. In fact, you can make assignments to have different club members update it for different periods. They can add news, events, facts, ask provocative questions, and more.

Talk about race. One goal could be to take some time to talk openly and nonjudgmentally about race. Learning to talk honestly about race—and creating a space where people of good will can ask honest questions—can be healing even when it's hard, while not talking about it can be toxic. If you feel uncomfortable or ill equipped to tackle such a difficult subject, you are not alone. Fortunately, there are many ways to address the crisis; choose your own angle. Here are some resources to help you get started.

Teaching Tolerance (TeachingTolerance.org). This site, run by the Southern Poverty Law Center, has a wealth of ideas, activities, and information that students, teachers, and clubs can use to promote racial fairness.

Not in Our Schools (niot.org/nios). The Not in Our Schools section of the organization Not in Our Town has dozens of age-appropriate activities and sources of information.

The National Education Campaign To End Racial Profiling (nea.org/home/52285.htm). The National Education Campaign To End Racial Profiling is a rich source of tips, lessons, and resources. It includes a one-page handout to inform students about racial profiling that any group or individual could use. It also has a shorter version of the Bust Card that reminds young people of their rights. The National Education Association (NEA) worked with a number of anti-hate organizations to develop the curriculum, which involves many different ways of actively addressing racism.

The NAACP's "Born Suspect" Report (naacp.org/pages/racialprofiling). Get involved with the NAACP's efforts to end racial profiling. Read "Born Suspect," a report about racial profiling, and view their sample End Racial Profiling Act.

Racial profiling will not end until young people like you get involved. Amy Hunter, whose son Ashton was racially profiled at age twelve, says, "Children should protest, should continue to ask for equity, should demand that injustice ends everywhere. Successful movements have been led by the young. If we are going to change this world we will need them to be brave, bold and definitely protesting."[9]

Progress is coming slowly, but one day, it will come. As Martin Luther King Jr. said, "The moral arc of the universe bends toward justice."

Chapter Notes

Chapter 1: The Talk
1. Hunter, Amy. Personal interview. August 15, 2015.
2. Obama, Barack. "Remarks by the President at the NAACP Conference." July 14, 2015. Retrieved September 8, 2015 (https://www.whitehouse.gov/the-press-office/2015/07/14/remarks-president-naacp-conference).
3. Chen, Joie. "5 things that may surprise you about Native Americans' police encounters." *Al Jazeera America,* January 27, 2015. Retrieved September 10, 2015 (http://america.aljazeera.com/watch/shows/america-tonight/articles/2015/1/27/things-that-may-surprise-you-about-native-americans-police-encounters.html).
4. "Who Are Police Killing?" Center on Juvenile and Criminal Justice, August 24, 2014. Retrievd September 1, 2015 (http://www.cjcj.org/news/8113).
5. Almasy, Steve. "Baltimore Mom who Slapped Son: He was Embarrassing Himself." CNN, April 29, 2015. Retrieved August 30, 2015 (http://www.cnn.com/2015/04/29/us/baltimore-mother-slapping-son/).
6. Associated Press, "Baltimore city jail refused to admit nearly 2,600 injured suspects, casting doubt on police tactics: report." *New York Daily News*, May 11, 2015. Retrieved August 9, 2015 (http://www.nydailynews.com/news/crime/2-500-people-injuries-baltimore-jail-article-1.2217561).
7. Douglas, Richard. "How Martin O'Malley Created Today's Baltimore." *The National Review,* May 6, 2015 (http://www.nationalreview.com/article/417958/how-martin-omalley-created-todays-baltimore-richard-j-douglas).
8. Hunter, Amy.

Chapter 2: What Is Racial Profiling?
1. Williams, Jonathan. Personal interview. August 18, 2015.

Chapter Notes

2. Webby, Sean. "San Jose police change definition of 'racial profiling.'" *San Jose Mercury News,* February 21, 2011. Retrieved August 21, 2015 (http://www.mercurynews.com/ci_17445138).
3. Rubin, Joel. "LAPD officer profiled Latinos in traffic stops, internal probe concludes." *Los Angeles Times,* March 27, 2012. Retrieved September 2, 2015 (http://articles.latimes.com/2012/mar/27/local/la-me-lapd-racial-profile-20120326).
4. Ibid.
5. Epp, Charles, and Steven Maynard-Moody. "Driving While Black." *Washington Monthly,* January/February 2014. Retrieved September 11, 2015 (http://www.washingtonmonthly.com/magazine/january_february_2014/ten_miles_square/driving_while_black048283.php?page=all).
6. Sehgal, Ujala. "Mapping Muslims: NYPD Spying and its Impact on American Muslims." Asian American Legal Defense and Education Fund, March 11, 2013. Retrieved August 7, 2015 (http://aaldef.org/press-releases/press-release/new-report-launched-nypd-spyings-impact-on-american-muslims.html).
7. Ibid.
8. Ibid.
9. Ibid.
10. Warikoo, Niraj. "State Police to investigate report of racial profiling during traffic stop." *Detroit Free Press,* March 22, 2012. Retrieved September 1, 2015 (http://archive.freep.com/article/20120322/NEWS05/203220448/State-Police-to-investigate-report-of-racial-profiling-during-traffic-stop).
11. McCarthy, Justin. "Immigrant Status Tied to Discrimination Among Hispanics." Gallup, August 20, 2015. Retrieved September 2, 2015 (http://www.gallup.com/poll/184769/immigrant-status-tied-discrimination-among-hispanics.aspx).

Chapter 3: On the Street

1. Coffey, Wayne, Tina Moore, and Larry McShane. "James Blake, former tennis star, slammed to ground and handcuffed outside midtown hotel by white NYPD cops who mistook him for ID theft suspect." *New York Daily News*, September 10, 2015. Retrieved

Are You Being Racially Profiled?

September 12, 2015 (http://www.nydailynews.com/sports/more-sports/ex-tennis-star-james-blake-mistakenly-tackled-white-cops-article-1.2353983).

2. Tracy, Thomas, Dareh Gregorian, Rachelle Blidner, and Corky Siemaszko. "NYPD cop who tackled tennis star James Blake has been sued 4 times for excessive force." *New York Daily News*, September 11, 2015. Retrieved September 14, 2015 (http://www.nydailynews.com/news/national/tackled-james-blake-sued-4-times-excessive-force-article-1.2356691).
3. New York Civil Liberties Union. "Stop-and-Frisk Data." Retrieved August 20, 2015 (http://www.nyclu.org/content/stop-and-frisk-data).
4. Williams, Jonathan. Personal interview. August 18, 2015.
5. Shockley, Madison T., II. "My Family Has Been Racially Profiled Everywhere from Harvard to Our Own Home." *The World Post*, October 28, 2014. Retrieved August 21, 2015 (http://www.huffingtonpost.com/madison-t-shockley-ii/family-racially-profiled-harvard_b_5724260.html).
6. Blow, Charles M. "Library Visit, Then Held at Gunpoint." *The New York Times,* January 26, 2015. Retrieved August 13, 2015 (www.nytimes.com/2015/01/26/opinion/charles-blow-at-yale-the-police-detained-my-son.html?_r=1).
7. Carson, Dale C., and Wes Denham. *Arrest-Proof Yourself: An Ex-Cop Reveals How Easy It Is for Anyone to Get Arrested, How Even a Single Arrest Could Ruin Your Life, and What to Do If the Police Get in Your Face.* Chicago, IL: Chicago Review Press, 2007.
8. Zaya, Alexandra, and Kameel Stanley. "How riding your bike can land you in trouble with the cops — if you're black." *Tampa Bay Times,* April 17, 2015. Retrieved September 2, 2015 (http://www.tampabay.com/news/publicsafety/how-riding-your-bike-can-land-you-in-trouble-with-the-cops---if-youre-black/2225966).

Chapter 4: Racial Profiling in Cars and Planes

1. Landau, Alex, and Patsy Hathaway. "I was just another black face in the streets." *StoryCorps.* Retrieved August 29, 2015 (https://storycorps.org/listen/alex-landau-and-patsy-hathaway/#).

2. "Traffic Stops." Bureau of Justice Statistics. Retrieved August 20, 2015 (http://www.bjs.gov/index.cfm?ty=tp&tid=702).
3. Williams, Stereo. "Chris Rock, Isaiah Washington, and Racial Profiling: Why Black People Shouldn't Have to 'Adapt'" *The Daily Beast,* April 20, 2015 (http://www.thedailybeast.com/articles/2015/04/02/chris-rock-isaiah-washington-and-racial-profiling-why-black-people-shouldn-t-have-to-adapt.html).
4. Pomper, Steve. *Is there a Problem Officer? A Cop's Inside Scoop on Avoiding Traffic Tickets.* Guilford, CT: Lyons Press, 2007.
5. Ahmad, Tahera, Facebook post, May 29, 2015 (https://www.facebook.com/tahera.ahmad.5/posts/10152815402232001).
6. American Civil Liberties Union, "What to do if you think you're on a no-fly list (https://www.aclu.org/know-your-rights/what-do-if-you-think-youre-no-fly-list).
7. Hastings, Deborah. "FBI put US Muslims on no-fly list to coerce them to become informants: lawsuit." *New York Daily News,* April 23, 2014. Retrieved August 14, 2015 (http://www.nydailynews.com/news/national/federal-lawsuit-claims-american-muslims-put-no-fly-list-coerced-informants-article-1.1766315).

Chapter 5: The School to Prison Pipeline

1. Moser, Laura. "This Florida Teenager Knows What Ahmed Mohamed Is Going Through. It Happened to Her in 2013." *Slate,* September 17, 2015. Retrieved September 18, 2015 (http://www.slate.com/blogs/schooled/2015/09/17/kiera_wilmot_arrest_florida_teenager_reacts_to_ahmed_mohamed_story.html).
2. Welsh, Jennifer. "Lawyer For Teen Arrested For A Science Experiment Working To Prevent Felony Charges From Being Filed." *Business Insider,* May 3, 2013. Retrieved July 28, 2015 (http://www.businessinsider.com/kiera-wilmot-lawyer-hoping-to-prevent-felony-charges-from-being-filed-2013-5).
3. Lewin, Tamar. "Black Students Face More Discipline, Data Suggests." *The New York Times,* March 6, 2012. Retrieved August 12, 2015 (http://www.nytimes.com/2012/03/06/education/black-students-face-more-harsh-discipline-data-shows.html).
4. Prupis, Nadia. "Black Girls Matter: Report Exposes Systemic

Oppression of Often-Ignored Groups." *Common Dreams,* February 5, 2015. Retrieved August 28, 2015 (http://www.commondreams.org/news/2015/02/05/black-girls-matter-report-exposes-systemic-oppression-often-ignored-groups).

5. McComb, Allegra. "Stanford researchers reveal teachers more likely to label black students 'troublemakers.'" *The Stanford Daily,* May 7, 2015. Retrieved August 22, 2015. (http://www.stanforddaily.com/2015/05/07/stanford-researchers-reveal-teachers-more-likely-to-label-black-students-troublemakers/).

6. Gross, Allie. "The Zero Tolerance Trap: How a policy meant to protect a school can ruin students' lives." *Slate,* October 13, 2014. Retrieved August 23, 2015 (http://www.slate.com/articles/life/education/2014/10/atiya_haynes_case_zero_tolerance_school_choice_and_one_detroit_student_s.html).

7. Milhiser, Ian. "American Schools Are More Segregated Now Than They Were in 1968, and the Supreme Court Doesn't Care" Think Progress, August 13, 2015. Retrieved October 1, 2015 (http://thinkprogress.org/justice/2015/08/13/3690012/american-schools-are-more-segregated-now-then-they-were-in-1968-and-the-supreme-court-doesnt-care/).

8. Michalowicz, Claire. "Mom of boy Tasered in high school cafeteria files lawsuit (documents)." *The Middletown Press,* June 14, 2011. Retrieved August 11, 2015 (http://www.middletownpress.com/general-news/20110614/mom-of-boy-tasered-in-high-school-cafeteria-files-lawsuit-documents).

9. "Discrimination against Students of Color Rampant in Louisiana School District." Southern Poverty Law Center, May 7, 2015. Retrieved August 8, 2015 (https://www.splcenter.org/news/2015/05/08/discrimination-against-students-color-rampant-louisiana-school-district).

10. Gee, Robyn. "Calif. Schools Try Out A Gentler Form Of Discipline." *Youth Radio,* June 6, 2012 (http://www.npr.org/2012/06/07/154461878/calif-school-district-finds-gentler-path-to-discipline).

Chapter Notes

Chapter 6: Police Overreach?

1. Jones, Jeffrey. "Urban Blacks in U.S. Have Little Confidence in Police." Gallup, December 8, 2014. Retrieved August 30, 2015 (http://www.gallup.com/poll/179909/urban-blacks-little-confidence-police.aspx).
2. H., Moses. Personal Interview. August 31, 2015.
3. Burke, Peter. "Pembroke Pines police officer refused service at Arby's." local10.com, September 2, 2015. Retrieved September 5, 2015 (http://www.local10.com/news/pembroke-pines-police-officer-refused-service-at-arbys/35060020f).
4. Berman, Mark. "Police officers experience fewer deaths these days — but increased tension." *The Washington Post*, May 30, 2015. Retrieved August 30, 2015 (https://www.washingtonpost.com/national/for-police-officers-fewer-deaths-but-increased-tension/2015/05/30/499da608-0650-11e5-8bda-c7b4e9a8f7ac_story.html).
5. Sallah, Michael. "Aggressive police take hundreds of millions of dollars from motorists not charged with crime." *The Washington Post*, September 6, 2014. Retrieved September 7, 2015 (http://www.washingtonpost.com/sf/investigative/2014/09/06/stop-and-seize/).
6. Balko, Radley. "Once again: police work is NOT getting more dangerous." *The Washington Post*, October 2, 2014. Retrieved September 8, 2015 (https://www.washingtonpost.com/news/the-watch/wp/2014/10/02/once-again-police-work-is-not-getting-more-dangerous).
7. Burton, Paul. "SWAT Team Raids Wrong Worcester Home, Residents Say." WBZ-TV, August 22, 2015. Retrieved September 8, 2015 (http://boston.cbslocal.com/2015/08/22/swat-team-raids-wrong-worcester-home-residents-say/).
8. "War Comes Home: The Excessive Militarization of American Policing." American Civil Liberties Union. Retrieved 22 July, 2015 (https://www.aclu.org/feature/war-comes-home?redirect=war-comes-home-excessive-militarization-american-policing).
9. Balko, Radley. "Once again: police work is NOT getting more dangerous." *The Washington Post*, October 2, 2014. Retrieved October 11, 2015 (https://www.washingtonpost.com/news/the-watch/wp/2014/10/02/once-again-police-work-is-not-getting-more-dangerous/).

10. Bier, Daniel. "Overkill: Militarizing America." Foundation for Economic Education. *The Freeman,* September 15, 2015 (http://fee.org/freeman/overkill-militarizing-america/).
11. Lind, William S. "Cops With War Toys." *The American Conservative,* August 22, 2014. Retrieved August 29, 2015 (http://www.theamericanconservative.com/articles/cops-with-war-toys/).
12. "The Counted: People Killed in the U.S. by Police in 2015." *The Guardian.* Retrieved September 10, 2015 (http://www.theguardian.com/us-news/series/counted-us-police-killings).
13. Kindy, Kimberly and Kimbriell Kelly. "Thousands Dead, Few Prosecuted." *Washington Post,* April 11, 2015. Retrieved August 31, 2015 (http://www.washingtonpost.com/sf/investigative/2015/04/11/thousands-dead-few-prosecuted/).
14. Neyfakh, Leon, and Aaron Wolfe. "That's Our Standard in Policing … Fear." *Slate,* August 6, 2015. Retrieved August 30, 2015 (http://www.slate.com/articles/news_and_politics/crime/2015/08/baltimore_ex_cop_discusses_police_violence_toward_young_black_men.html).
15. Tomlinson, Stuart. "Clatskanie officer who filed racism complaint against chief receives death threats." *The Oregonian,* September 8, 2015. Retrieved September 14, 2015 (http://www.oregonlive.com/pacific-northwest-news/index.ssf/2015/0/clatskanie_officer_who_filed_r.html).

Chapter 7: Juvenile Injustice

1. Ford, Dana. "Man jailed as teen without conviction commits suicide." CNN, June 15, 2015. Retrieved August 21, 2015 (http://www.cnn.com/2015/06/07/us/kalief-browder-dead/).
2. Feriss, Susan. "Juvenile Injustice: Truants Face Courts, Jailing without Legal Counsel to Aid Them." The Center for Public Integrity, June 16, 2015. Retrieved August 30, 2015 (http://www.publicintegrity.org/2014/05/09/14699/juvenile-injustice-truants-face-courts-jailing-without-legal-counsel-aid-them).
3. Feriss, Susan. "Juvenile Injustice: Truants Face Courts, Jailing without Legal Counsel to Aid Them." The Center for Public Integrity, June 16, 2015. Retrieved August 30, 2015 (http://www.publicintegrity.

Chapter Notes

org/2014/05/09/14699/juvenile-injustice-truants-face-courts-jailing-without-legal-counsel-aid-them).

4. Friedman, Benjamin. "Protecting Truth: An Argument for Juvenile Rights and a Return to In re Gault." *UCLA Law Review*. Retrieved September 3, 2015 (http://www.uclalawreview.org/protecting-truth-an-argument-for-juvenile-rights-and-a-return-to-in-re-gault/).
5. "What are the causes and effects of racial profiling, and what can we do about it?" The Ella Baker Center. *Heal the Streets 2011 Participatory Action Research Report, 2011*. Retrieved September 1, 2015 (http://ellabakercenter.org/sites/default/files/downloads/hts_racial_profiling_report_2011.pdf).

Chapter 8: Prisons

1. Criminal Justice Fact Sheet. NAACP. Retrieved August 29, 2015 (http://www.naacp.org/pages/criminal-justice-fact-sheet).
2. Kroll, Andy. "This Is How Private Prison Companies Make Millions Even When Crime Rates Fall." *Mother Jones*, September 19, 2013. Retrieved August 3, 2015 (http://www.motherjones.com/mojo/2013/09/private-prisons-occupancy-quota-cca-crime).
3. Alexander, Michelle. *The New Jim Crow: Mass Incarceration in the Age of Colorblindness*. New York, NY: New Press, 2010.
4. Rehavi, M. Marit, and Sonja B. Starr. "Racial Disparity in Federal Criminal Sentences." *Journal of Political Economy*, 122.6. (2014): n. pag. Retrieved August 22, 2015 (http://econ.sites.olt.ubc.ca/files/2015/01/pdf_paper_marit-rehavi-racial_disparity.pdf).
5. Michaelson, Jay. "95% of Prosecutors Are White and They Treat Blacks Worse." *The Daily Beast*, August 17, 2015. Retrieved August 29, 2015 (http://www.thedailybeast.com/articles/2015/08/17/95-of-prosecutors-are-white-and-they-treat-blacks-worse.html).
6. Kerby, Sophia. "The Top 10 Most Startling Facts About People of Color and Criminal Justice in the United States." Center for American Progress, March 13, 2012. Retrieved August 20, 2015 (https://www.americanprogress.org/issues/race/news/2012/03/13/11351/the-top-10-most-startling-facts-about-people-of-color-and-criminal-justice-in-the-united-states/).
7. "Prop 6: Amending California's Three Strikes Law." *San Diego Free*

Press, September 4, 2012. Retrieved September 3, 2015 (http://sandiegofreepress.org/2012/09/prop-36-amending-californias-three-strikes-law/).

8. Taibbi, Matt. "Cruel and Unusual Punishment: The Shame of Three Strikes Laws." *Rolling Stone,* March 27, 2013. Retrieved September 1, 2015 (http://www.rollingstone.com/politics/news/cruel-and-unusual-punishment-the-shame-of-three-strikes-laws-20130327).

9. Sledge, Matt. "The Drug War And Mass Incarceration By The Numbers." *The Huffington Post,* April 8, 2013. Retrieved August 28, 2015 (http://www.huffingtonpost.com/2013/04/08/drug-war-mass-incarceration_n_3034310.html).

10. Barclay, Jasmine. "Mass Incarceration Has Affected Me My Whole Life." *The Huffington Post*, December 15, 2014. Retrieved August 11, 2015 (http://www.huffingtonpost.com/jasmine-barclay/mass-incarceration-has-af_b_6327872.html).

11. Drug War Statistics. Drug Policy Alliance. Retrieved August 30, 2015 (http://www.drugpolicy.org/drug-war-statistics).

12. Zornick, George. "Rick Perry at CPAC Panel on Criminal Justice: 'Shut Prisons Down. Save That Money.'" *The Nation*, March 7, 2015. Retrieved August 1, 2015 (http://www.thenation.com/article/rick-perry-cpac-panel-criminal-justice-shut-prisons-down-save-money/).

Chapter 9: Fighting Against Racial Profiling

1. Jane (Name has been changed). Personal Interview. August 31, 2015.
2. King, Shaun. (@ShaunKing). "If you ever wondered what it would be like to live in the Civil Rights Movement, and what role you would play, you are in it right now." August 12, 2015. Tweet.
3. "Survey finds youth use new media for peer-based participatory politics." *UChicagoNews,* June 27, 2012. Retrieved September 10, 2015 (http://news.uchicago.edu/article/2012/06/27/survey-finds-youth-use-new-media-peer-based-participatory-politics).
4. Naughton, John "Rewire by Ethan Zuckerman; Untangling the Web by Aleks Krotoski – review." *The Guardian,* July 21, 2013. Retrieved August 31, 2015 (http://www.theguardian.com/books/2013/jul/21/rewire-zuckerman-untangling-krotoski-review).
5. Day, Elizabeth. "#BlackLivesMatter: the birth of a new civil rights

Chapter Notes

movement." *The Guardian,* July 19, 2015. Retrieved September 8, 2015 (http://www.theguardian.com/world/2015/jul/19/blacklivesmatter-birth-civil-rights-movement).
6. Ibid.
7. Wolfson, Todd. *Digital Rebellion: The Birth of the Cyber Left.* Chicago, IL: University of Illinois Press, 2014.
8. Desmond-Harris, Jenee. "The only good news about the McKinney pool party is the white kids' response to racism." *Vox Media,* June 9, 2015. Retrieved August 30, 2015.
9. Hunter, Amy. Personal interview. August 15, 2015.

Glossary

adversarial—A system of justice marked by the opposition of the prosecution and the defense.

arraigned—To be called before a court to hear the charges against a person.

arrest—To seize a person and take him or her into police custody, or control.

bond card—A card that police may be willing to accept instead of a driver's license as a way to guarantee that the person will pay for a speeding or other ticket.

commute—To reduce the severity of a judicial sentence.

discrimination—Unjust treatment of an individual or group based on prejudice.

ethnic—Relating to a group of people having a common national or cultural tradition.

expulsion—When a student is kicked out of school as a punishment.

expunge—To remove something, such as a criminal charge, from a person's record.

harass—To annoy, disturb, or pick on someone.

implicit bias—Attitudes that affect our understanding and actions that are a result of subconscious prejudices.

Glossary

intolerance—An unwillingness to recognize and respect differences in other people's views and beliefs.

mandatory minimum—A sentencing guideline that requires judges to give a defendant a harsh sentence even if there are reasons that might have otherwise made the judge give a smaller penalty.

prejudice—Hatred for others based on race, ethnicity, or nationality.

probable cause—When police suspect a person may have committed a crime.

racial profiling—A practice in which government agents, such as police and judges, treat members of minorities differently on the basis of their race.

racism—A belief that people of different races are inferior; this belief is usually against people who belong to other racial groups.

reasonable suspicion—When police suspect you are about to commit a crime.

resilience—The ability to bounce back from a traumatic event.

stop and frisk—A policy under which police make random stops, interrogations, and searches even without cause or suspicion.

suspension—When a student is forbidden to go to school for a period of time as a punishment.

zero tolerance policy—System used in many schools for punishing any and every infraction regardless of intent, circumstances, or human error.

For More Information

The Advancement Project
1220 L Street NW, Suite 850
Washington, DC 20005
202-728-9557
advancementproject.org

American Civil Liberties Union
125 Broad Street, 18th Floor
New York NY 10004
212-549-2500
ACLU.org

American Immigration Council
1331 G St. NW, Suite 200
Washington, DC 20005
202-507-7500
americanimmigrationcouncil.org

Amnesty International USA
5 Penn Plaza
New York, NY 10001
212-807-8400
amnestyusa.org

Canadian Anti-racism Education and Research Society (CAERS)
210-124 East Pender Street
Vancouver, BC V3T 4E3
Canada
604-687-7350

For More Information

stopracism.ca/content/canadian-anti-racism-education-and-research-society-caers

Canadian Race Relations Foundation
6 Garamond Court, Suite 225
Toronto, Ontario M3C 1Z5
Canada
416-441-1900
crr.ca/en

Islamic Networks Group
3031 Tisch Way, Suite 950
San Jose, CA 95128
408-296-7312
ing.org

The Leadership Conference on Civil and Human Rights
1629 K Street NW, 10th Floor
Washington, DC 20006
202-466-3311
civilrights.org

National Association for the Advancement of Colored People (NAACP)
4805 Mt. Hope Drive
Baltimore, MD 21215
877-NAACP-98
naacp.org

Southern Poverty Law Center
400 Washington Ave.
Montgomery, AL 36104
334-956-8200
splcenter.org

Are You Being Racially Profiled?

Websites

Lawyer's Committee for Civil Rights Under Law

lawyerscommittee.org/project/educational-opportunities-project

Organization dedicated to ensuring that all students receive equal educational opportunities in public schools.

National Urban League

nul.org

Dedicated to stengthening communities and ensuring equal opportunites for jobs, education, healthcare, and housing.

Understanding Prejudice

understandingprejudice.org/links/reducing.html

Provides resources and links to educate and comprehend prejudice in the United States.

Further Reading

Bryfonski, Dedria. *Islamophobia.* Farmington Hills, Mich.: Greenhaven Press. 2012.

Coates, Ta-Nahesi. *Between the World and Me.* New York: Random House, 2015.

Hanson-Harding, Alexandra. *I've Been Racially Profiled, Now What?* (Now What?) New York: Rosen Publishing, 2014.

Mauer, Marc and Sabrina Jones. *Race to Incarcerate: A Graphic Retelling.* New York: The New Press. 2013.

Palmer, Libbi. *The PTSD Workbook for Teens: Simple, Effective Skills for Healing Traumas.* Oakland, Calif.: New Harbinger Publications, Inc. 2012.

Thomas, Bonnie. *Creative Expression Activities for Teens: Exploring Identity through Art, Craft and Journaling.* Philadelphia, Pa.: Jessica Kingsley Publishers. 2011.

Index

A
ACLU's Know Your Rights wallet card, 31
Ahmad, Tahera, 40–42
Al Jazeera, 7
Al Qaeda, 18
American Conservative, The, 62–63
American Civil Liberties Union (ACLU), 15, 21, 31, 43, 44, 60, 84
Arab Spring, 91

B
bail, 67–69
Balfaz, Robert, 45
Balko, Radley, 60, 62
Baltimore, Maryland, 8–10, 63, 86, 89, 91
Baltimore Sun, The, 8–10
Bartow, Florida, 44
biking laws, 31–33
Black Lives Matter, 89–90
Blake, James, 23–24
Blow, Charles M., 27
Bratton, William, 16
Briceno, Tiburcio, 21 Brooklyn, New York, 56
Browder, Kalief, 66–67
Business Insider, 44–45

C
cameras, 11, 38
Carson, Dale, 29
Civil Right Movement, 13, 86–88
Columbia University, 45
Cordell, LaDoris, 16
court appointment lawyers, 70–72

D
Daily News, 24
Davis, Eric, 33
Denver, Colorado, 34
driving, 36–38
  if stopped while, 38–40

E
Eagle, Karen, 7
expunging a record, 75

F
FBI, 18–20, 31, 43,
Fifth Amendment, 18
finding a lawyer, 30–31
Fourteenth Amendment, 18, 43
Fourth Amendment, 18
Foxx, Jamie, 36

G
Graham, Toya, 8
Gray, Freddie, 8–10, 91

Index

H
Hardaway, Larry, 44–45
Harris, David, 63
Harvard University, 27
Hashmi, Faisal, 21
Haynes, Atiya, 47
hijab, 40
Hoover, Marvin, 65
Huffington Post, 27
Hunter, Amy, 4–5, 13, 93

I
Immigration and Naturalization Service (INS), 21
implicit bias, 45–47
Islamic State (ISIS), 20

J
Jackson, Zahrod, 49–50
juvenile justice, 50, 67

K
King Jr., Martin Luther, 93

L
Landau, Alex, 34–36
Lind, William, 62
Livonia, Michigan, 21
Los Angeles Police Department (LAPD), 16

M
mandatory minimums, 79–82, 83–84
"Mapping Muslims: NYPD Spying and its Impacts on American Muslims," 20–21
Martin, Trayvon, 89

N
New Jim Crow, The, 79, 88
New York City, 20, 23, 56, 66
New York Civil Liberties Union, 25
New York Police Department (NYPD), 20, 25
New York Times, 27
Nixon, Richard, 58, 79
No Fly List, 43
NOLO, 31

O
Obama, Barack, 7, 83–84
Okonofua, Jason, 47
O'Malley, Martin, 10
Overseas Citizen Service, 43

P
pedestrian laws, 27
Perry, Rick, 83
plea deals, 69, 80
   being wary of, 72
police
   attitudes toward, 55–58
   community and, 65
   in schools, 49
   issues within, 63–65
   militarization of, 58–60
   war on, 60–63
police killings of civilians, 63
   African Americans, 7, 8–10
   Freddie Gray, 8–10
   Michael Brown, 91
   Native Americans, 7
Pomper, Steve, 38

Prison-Industrial Complex, 11, 76–79
Pushed Out, Overpoliced and Underprotected, 45

R

racial profiling
  African Americans, of, 4–5, 7, 18, 23–24, 25, 31–33, 36, 60, 79–80
  avoiding, 27–29
  definition, 7, 15
  drug crime and, 79
  fighting against, 85–93
  in schools, 45–47
  Latino Americans, of, 21–22, 36, 43, 60, 79
  Muslim Americans, of, 18–21, 40–43
  Native Americans, of, 7, 22
  police departments and, 15–16, 18, 20–22, 23–27, 31–33
  problem with, 18
  social media as a weapon against, 42, 54, 88–90
  what to do if you are, 30
  while driving, 36–38
  while flying, 40–43
restorative justice, 75
Rock, Chris, 36
rough rides, 8–10

S

Sama, Ahsan, 21
San Jose, California, 15–16
Scaglione, Anthony, 58
school regulations, 50–54
school suspensions, 44–45
segregation, 49–50

September 11, 2001, 18, 20, 58
Shockley II, Madison, 27
Smith, Patrick, 16
Special Weapons and Tactics (SWAT), 60
status offenses, 70
stereotyping, 47, 88
St. Louis, Missouri, 4
Stone, Alex, 63–64
stop and frisk, 24–27
StoryCorps, 36

T

Tampa, Florida, 31
Tampa Bay Times, 31
teenage brain, 69–70
three-strikes law, 80–82, 83

U

US Constitution, 11, 18, 43, 52
US Customs and Border Protection, 21
US Department of Education, 45
US Justice Department, 16, 36, 79

W

War on Drugs, 58, 79, 83
War on Terror, 58
Williams, Jonathan, 14–15, 25
Wilmot, Kiera, 44–45
Woods, Michael, 63
World Trade Center, 58

Y

Yale University, 16, 27

Z

zero tolerance policies, 47